In the Shadows of the Birch Trees

Jeremy Bending spent his life as a hospital doctor and consultant physician. During that time, in addition to writing numerous medical and scientific papers, he continued to write fiction and stories. Some of these were brought together in his book *A Listening Doctor,* published in 2018. His first novel, *In the Shadows of the Birch Trees,* tells the story of a young Hungarian woman Eszter who, by an extraordinary twist of fate, escapes with her baby Eva from the horror of the mass killings taking place in WW2, in Birkenau, as they are about to enter the extermination camp. The story of their lives following this reprieve – and that of the SS guard Peter Leahy who allowed them to escape – includes the flight of Eszter and Eva from Budapest before the Soviet invasion in 1956, and the life Eva makes for herself subsequently. Eva meets up with Peter many years later and discovers that her mother and he both lived their lives regretting their lost love of each other. At the age of seventy, now an eminent researcher into eye disease, Eva herself goes blind.

By the same Author –

A Listening Doctor

In the Shadows of
the Birch Trees

Jeremy Bending

Arena Books

First published in 2020 by Arena Books

Arena Books
6 Southgate Green
Bury St. Edmunds
IP33 2BL

www.arenabooks.co.uk

*Distributed in America by Ingram International, One Ingram Blvd., P.O. Box 3006,
La Vergne, TN 37086-1985, USA.*

Jeremy Bending
In the Shadows of the Birch Trees

British Library cataloguing in Publication Data. A Catalogue record
for this book is available from the British Library.

ISBN-13   978-1-911593-71-3

BIC classifications:- FA, FJMS, FRD.

Cover design
by Jason Anscomb

Typeset in
Times New Roman

To Jan

' . . . in all the Lagers the flight of even a single prisoner was considered the most grievous fault on the part of the surveillance personnel, beginning with the functionary-prisoners and ending with the camp commander, who risked being discharged. In Nazi logic, this was an intolerable event: the escape of a slave, especially a slave belonging to races 'of inferior biological value', seemed to be charged with symbolic value, would represent a victory by one who by definition is defeated, a shattering of the myth; more realistically, it was also an objective damage since every prisoner had seen things that the world must not know,'

Primo Levi, *The Drowned and the Saved,* Simon & Schuster, Inc. 1988, p. 125.

'Many times man lives and dies
Between his two eternities . . .
Whether man die in his bed
Or a rifle knocks him dead,
A brief parting from those dear
Is the worst man has to fear.'

W.B. Yeats, *Under Ben Bulben,*
Collected Poems, Macmillan 1933.

CHAPTER 1

The feeling that she was somehow different from those around her had been with Eva since she was a young child. She was sure that the feeling was not something she had imagined or manufactured, but just something the existence of which she'd been aware of for as long as she could remember. It did not cause her any discomfort, but did continue to bemuse her from time to time when the feeling bubbled to the surface. When she was old enough to have insight into the fact that she had this feeling and reflect on its existence, she was clear in her mind that this had not grown out of arrogance or self-importance: these were not characteristics which she had ever possessed or would ever develop.

Eva's conviction of 'otherness' also had nothing to do with the fact that she was Jewish by birth. She had actually been brought up and lived in a largely secular society. Her mother Eszter, although born into a strict Jewish family, had been a non-practising Jew for all the years that Eva was with her. But although Eva was not to know this as a young child, her and her mother's Jewishness, or perceived lack of it, was to determine her survival when she was only a young baby.

Her mother told Eva the story of her escape from death at a very early age when she was about eleven. Eszter's father had been a prominent professor of medicine at the Semmelweis University in Budapest for over twenty years and the family were well-known and held in high regard in the city. This had not prevented them from being reported to the occupying Germans as Jews by their long-standing neighbours, Gabor Szabo and his wife Klara, themselves professional people, who were both teachers. As a result, Eszter's parents and their whole family had been arrested at gunpoint by the Gestapo late one night and taken away by force from their family apartment in the centre of Budapest. Her mother Eszter told her how she had been dragged by the Gestapo thugs into the street and onto a truck, screaming for the life of her baby Eva to be saved, and later loaded by force and at gunpoint onto the death train with her young baby, along with her mother and father, sister and aunt.

They were held imprisoned on the train for what seemed like weeks. There were about eighty men, women and children of all ages packed into their cattle wagon alone, such that there was hardly room for a person to stand, let alone to find space to lie down. From time to time, one or other of them was able to sit for a short while by taking turns with those around them. Most of those in the wagon were Hungarian Jews like themselves, and had been arrested and dragged from their homes without warning, interspersed with Roma gypsy families and men, women and children who were disabled either physically or mentally. There had been no stops for food or water or even toilet breaks during the entire journey, and they had shared what little water they had between each other. There was just a thin covering of straw on the floor. The wagon stank of excrement and disease, not to mention the stench of the decomposing bodies of the elderly, ill and disabled who had not survived the journey and lay around them on the floor of the wagon where they had died.

Their journey ended when the train eventually came to a stop at its final destination – the railhead to Birkenau concentration camp. The door to their wagon was thrown open and men with striped shirts and black trousers jumped in waving their truncheons in every direction, beating the people mercilessly as they forced them out of the truck. As her mother fell out of the railway wagon with baby Eva in her arms, they were helped up from the dust track onto which they had fallen by a young SS officer, who could not have been much more than twenty years old. He was blond and blue-eyed and did not seem to Eva's mother Eszter to have the hate in his eyes which she could see in all those other SS guards surrounding them. He'd looked at Eszter and her baby with a softness and kindness which was in stark contrast to the rough brutality of the other guards. 'You shouldn't be here,' he said quietly and with certainty to Eva's mother. They stood still, looking at each other for a few brief seconds, both of them ignoring the chaos all around them. Then, very gently, the soldier pushed them off to the side away from the throng of bedraggled people who were being forced down the path – men deemed to be able to work to the right, the rest being sent to the left to be gassed – by the other SS guards with their guns and their baying Alsatian dogs towards the 'showers'.

Eva's mother had never told her daughter the reason they had been spared. Could it really have been that the guard had decided that they didn't look Jewish, as her mother had implied? Or was it that the young soldier had taken a spontaneous attraction to her mother, perhaps the result of the fleeting physical contact that had occurred in that brief encounter; or had they survived as a result of an agreement that her mother had made, in that terrible moment, with this young man to repay him with more basic sexual favours if he would agree to release them? An agreement that Eva's mother would never have mentioned to her daughter, at whatever age, had it taken place.

Eva had never had the courage to ask her mother how it was they had been so very lucky, and her mother had never been inclined to go into more detail. The result was, however, that Eszter made her escape at the gates of the camp with her baby Eva in her arms, running off through the trees to freedom from death. A most vile death, as they were to learn later. That their luck was extraordinary was not in doubt.

Many years after the War, when Eva was an adult, she was able to research the facts. She read that the extermination camps of Auschwitz and Birkenau were to murder an estimated 1.5 million Jews, Roma and others with almost none of the condemned surviving to tell the story of their escape. This was true for Eszter's father, mother, sister and aunt who had all died in the gas chamber within no more than an hour after their arrival at the camps. More than 400,000 Hungarian Jews alone – half of the pre-war Jewish population of Hungary – were exterminated in Bunker II Birkenau between May and November 1944. Only about 144 prisoners are known to have escaped from Auschwitz, and most of those were from prisoners who escaped from worksites outside the camps where they were labouring at the time.

Eva also found the time to read books by some of those who had survived the Holocaust atrocities, including those of Elie Wiesel and Primo Levi. Amongst all his personal accounts of surviving the evil of Auschwitz and his highly intelligent dissection of the motives of the Nazi perpetrators of the Holocaust, Levi pointed out why prisoners were not allowed to escape under any circumstances: to allow just one do so would be to spread encouragement to others that this might also be possible for them, and also lead to the freedom into the outside world of men and women who had seen things that the world must not know.

But perhaps it was the fact that Eszter and her baby Eva were released from the lines of the condemned at the railhead before even reaching the path to the gas chambers which saved them? She knew she would probably never find out the truth.

CHAPTER 2

April, 2014

Walking around the centre of Krakow, although it was late on that April evening, the man and his wife came across many ticket offices still open to the tourist public. These were advertising day trips to Auschwitz and Birkenau and the prices of the various tours to the former concentration camps that were on offer. The tourist agencies existed in most of the main streets, as well as in smaller offices in many of the side streets and even in single rooms on the ground floors of minor alleys. They hesitated a long time, knowing that they should not have come all this way on holiday to southern Poland and go home without visiting the camps. Eventually they bought two tickets from a young man in a small office in an alley off one of the main streets who was about to shut up shop for the night.

The next morning they found themselves in one of dozens of coaches full of tourists who were being bussed backwards and forwards every day of the year to see the site of this appalling historic tragedy. Wilthord Leahy, their guide for their visit to the concentration camps of Auschwitz and Birkenau, was a young man in his early thirties. He met them off the coach from Krakow which had brought them to Auschwitz and introduced himself as their guide for the day. He was very polite, repeatedly addressing his group of about thirty visitors as 'Ladies and Gentlemen' in an American-English accent. He guided them around the camps expertly and spoke with precision about the bare statistics of the horrifying mass murder machine that had been designed, honed and 'perfected' by the Nazi command. The weather on the day of their visit was very hot and dry, but Wilthord, who worked as a senior guide to the camps of Auschwitz and Birkenau every day of the year and in all weathers, carried with him a short telescoped umbrella as well as wearing dark glasses at all times. But behind the sunglasses, it soon became clear that the guide not only had a deep knowledge of the horrible statistics of the Holocaust but also had an equally profound feeling for the immense pathos of the place.

Wilthord explained that many of the Jewish families who had been sent to their deaths in the extermination camps had actually been required to buy their own tickets for the train journey to Auschwitz, and had done so in the belief that this would be a chance to gain work and food in the camps once they had arrived there. The journey had thus been portrayed as an opportunity to start a new life away from the poverty war had brought for those who could afford it. This was just one example of the duplicity which the Germans had developed, which was aimed at keeping order and minimising dissent amongst the thousands of condemned people who were rounded up to be transported to their deaths. As the Nazi death machines became ever more 'perfected' other tricks had been introduced, such as the placing of comfortable armchairs at the railhead, at the point of arrival of the death trains, and the small orchestras which had been assembled to play music as the condemned were brought off the trains. The final trick of all had been the confiscation of all belongings – 'please remember where you have left your suitcases and mark the cases of your children with their names and date of birth' the prisoners were told on arrival – the removal of clothes and the shaving of heads, all in a pantomime to suggest that this was some sort of medical cleansing programme which was to end in the 'showers' to which the desperate people were then all led in to.

Wilthord guided their group into brick-block after brick-block which contained exhibits of horrors too terrible to imagine.

'Along this side of the room, Ladies and Gentlemen,' Wilthord explained as he led the group into another of the long blocks, 'you will find a glass cabinet the whole length of the room which contains only human hair.' He paused as his party spread themselves along the length of the cabinet and peered in at its grotesque contents.

'It is estimated that this collection alone represents the hair shaved from the heads of about 40,000 women prior to their gassing to death.' He paused again as the visitors took in the horror of this exhibit.

'Most of the hair which was shaved from the heads of the condemned,' Wilthord continued, 'was collected and transported back to factories in Germany where it was used as padding material in the manufacture of sofas, other soft furnishings and the like.'

He went on to state factually that the German company which had been involved in this macabre but highly lucrative business had prospered as a result of it and was still prospering to this day, nearly seventy years after the end of the War. As indeed, he told them, were many of the manufacturing, chemical, pharmaceutical and other companies which had prospered immensely from the War and which continued to be some of the richest companies in the world to the present day. Krupp, Siemens-Schuckert and IG Farben had relied in the 1940s on slave labour from concentration camps; the latter utilising 30,000 prisoners from Auschwitz as forced workers. One of IG Farben's subsidiaries supplied the poison gas, Zyklon B, that killed over one million people in the gas chambers during the Holocaust and IG Farben built factories in a sub camp in Monowitz near to Auschwitz (where the Italian prisoner Primo Levi was made to work), using the forced labour of the more robust prisoners as free labour before they too perished from starvation or disease.

As their party emerged back into the sunlight, blinking after the darkness of the dull light of the cell-blocks, Wilthord pointed out a large open trench about the size and shape of a swimming pool, near the blockhouses where Auschwitz prisoners were housed.

'During the war this was filled with water,' he said.

'Why was that?' a visitor asked him.

'Because it was required by the camp's fire insurance policy,' he replied.

The group of visitors let out an audible sound of air in disbelief. There was something grotesquely chilling about this information – that a camp whose purpose was mass extermination would, at the same time, concern itself with such a precaution and compliance with insurance law. And the company that insured the camp – Allianz – is still a major worldwide insurance company to this day, Wilthord went on to tell them.

At the end of the tour the husband and wife thanked Wilthord very much for his patience and empathy and asked him about how long he had been doing this job as tour guide to Auschwitz-Birkenau. He told them he had been doing so for eight years, since he had completed his university degree in political sociology. They told him what a very important job they thought he was doing, and asked him to keep on doing it. He accepted their thanks with a gracious bow of the head. It did not seem to them appropriate to tip him with money, as one American tourist had done already.

'Do you mind if I ask you what it was that prompted you to take on this role of guide to the extermination camps in the first place and continue it for so long?' the woman asked Wilthord, as the rest of the visitors were making their way back to the coaches to return to Krakow.

'My great-grandparents lived in the small Polish village of Brzezinka,' Wilthord replied. 'It was destroyed on the orders of the German occupying forces in 1941 in order to build the Auschwitz II concentration camp – Birkenau, where we are now standing – on the site where the village had been. They lost their home and nearly everything they owned during the forced evacuation, but by luck they were able to start a new life on a small farm only a short distance away from where the village used to be. My grandparents and then my parents continued to live on that farm after them. It was there that I was born and brought up.'

As they stood at the exit of Birkenau, Wilthord pointed over towards the woods, the other side of which his boyhood home, a small farm not far from where the demolished village of Brzezinka had been, was situated. The husband and wife walked together back to their coach. They could only guess how his upbringing and family history had led him to take on this role in his life.

As they sat in the back of the coach on the trip back to Krakow, the woman expressed her distaste for the commercialisation that had grown up around the Holocaust memorials. Two million visitors a year now came to Auschwitz, she had read. The whole enterprise seemed to have been somehow degraded by the modern wish to make it all into an 'attraction', she thought. Thank goodness that cameras and the taking of pictures – not to mention 'selfies' – were banned during the visits. She did at least acknowledge that she was aware that to this day all German secondary school pupils are required to visit Auschwitz on a school-arranged trip. She remained appalled, however, by the knowledge she had gained from German language students visiting England, to whom she taught English in the summer months, that the Holocaust atrocities were always blamed on 'the Nazis' rather than 'us Germans', in a palpable exercise if not to re-write history then at least to somehow sanitise it for this and future generations.

Sitting on the coach, watching the ordinary Polish countryside pass by out of the window, the man listened quietly to his wife's sentiments. But he knew he would remain forever overcome by the profound experience their visit had imprinted on him – in spite of the coachloads of hundreds of visitors – and the fact that, having born witness to the actuality of the crimes, nothing could ever again erase the memories of those crimes in his mind. He was certain that every leader of every nation in the world, and every aspiring leader, should be required to visit the place which is Auschwitz-Birkenau.

CHAPTER 3

July, 1944

'Go, go, go!' Eszter shouted to herself as she ran, jumping over rocks and concrete blocks. As she reached the electrified wire at the camp's boundary she caught a glimpse of a notice board on the fence post: Warning. Danger of Death. Undeterred, she did not stop but drove herself without hesitating towards the wire fence. A surge of severe pain hit her on the back of her left hand as her whole body was propelled forwards through the wire by a violent thunderbolt. As she picked herself up on the other side, she looked down and saw that her hand had been burnt by a vicious shock from the electrified fence as she had frantically forced a loose part of the wire aside to let herself and her baby through. The sound of the camp sirens was already blaring deafeningly in her ears and at that moment gunfire rang out from the camp's lookout towers. Hails of bullets shied off the rocks as the machine guns raked the ground around her. She didn't stop running for a second, weaving a zig-zag path to left and right. Miraculously, not one of the bullets hit their mark.

She ran across the waste ground on the other side of the electric fence and then slammed sideways into a bush like an American footballer into the opposing team, holding her baby tight inside her coat as she went. She fell out of the other side of the bush, cuts all over her arms and face from the brambles. She picked herself and her baby up from the ground and continued to sprint across the open scrubland towards the woods. As she sprinted the last few steps into the cover of the trees, she tripped flat on her face and landed hard on top of Eva as she did so. The baby let out a groan but at no time did she burst into wails of tears. Perhaps in some way she too sensed the mortal fear of her mother?

Eszter lay flat on her stomach for a few seconds, winded, and breathed heavily to regain her breath. As soon as she had done so, she staggered to her feet and made her way on through the heavy undergrowth of the wood; this time stumbling rather than running forward as fast as she could. The sound of the camp sirens faded gradually to a whine behind her and, eventually, stopped. When she was as deep into the woods as she could get, she rolled into a pit in the earth which was screened by surrounding bushes and lay there panting, pulling the damp undergrowth over them. She continued to clutch little Eva as close to her as she could. Her baby gave an occasionally little whimper, but even then did not cry out aloud. After a while, Eszter pulled a small piece of dry bread she had been saving out of her coat pocket. She tore the centre of it out for Eva to suck on, even though it was stale, and slowly chewed through the remaining crust herself. It was still early in the day, and Eszter knew they had to lie still where they were, waiting for nightfall before they could even think about finding their way out through the other side of the woods and into open country.

As she and her baby lay rigid in that damp ditch, Eva could hear the sound of soldiers searching the forest around them and the shouts of men pushing deeper into the forest away from them. She could also hear the frenzied barking of the Alsatian dogs. She listened in fear, praying that they would not be discovered and also praying that, if they were, they would not be found first by the dogs and ripped to death in the ditch where they were hiding. She lay there with her baby in that pit, falling in and out of a restless sleep, a sleep disturbed by horrible dreams of capture and death.

After many hours had passed, Eszter no longer heard the sounds of men searching for them and the dogs' barking; for some reason, the running feet and gunfire her dreams had foretold had never found them. Eventually she started to hope that perhaps the guards had abandoned their search: that the escape of a young girl and her baby had been written off by the camp guards as not worth bothering about for any longer. She guessed it was more likely that they had assumed that they would not get far; that it would be very easy for them to be picked up as they tried to escape through the wood into German occupied Poland. She fell back into a more peaceful sleep this time.

Eszter woke again later with the baby nuzzling at her breast through her coarse clothing. She unbuttoned her shirt and fed the baby what there was of her own milk. Not much, but the little there was, was nevertheless gratefully received. She pulled the shirt closed again, raised her head a little and looked around, listening intently. She could hear the noise of the occasional bird moving in the trees, but not once now did she hear the sound of soldiers crashing through the woods looking for them. She had no idea of the time, but the sky above was black and she could see an occasional star poking through the gaps at the tops of the trees. She knew it was night, and time for them to move on.

Eszter pulled herself to her feet, holding on to a branch of the bush above to give her leverage. Her whole body was stiff from the hours they had lain unmoving in the damp ditch and she was bruised and cut all over her arms and face from the brambles she had fallen through. There was an angry burn on the back of her right hand caused by the shock she had received from the electrified fence. Her right shoulder was bruised and throbbing with pain, the result of the impact it had taken as she'd crashed through the thick bushes to make her escape. Once she was standing, she climbed shakily out of the ditch with Eva still wrapped in her blanket inside her shirt. The blanket was soaked with the little girl's urine and faeces, but there was nothing her mother could do to clean the baby. She peered ahead of her into the woods and started to take tentative steps in what she thought might be the right direction to take them out to the other side. There was no moon and therefore almost no light for her to see by, but Eszter realised that this was probably to her advantage as she searched for the end of the wood, hauling herself along tree by tree.

After about thirty minutes struggling through the densely wooded undergrowth, stopping frequently to listen for sounds from any men that still might be hunting for them, Eszter could see the sky ahead more clearly, as the trees started to thin out. At last, she came to a ditch which she jumped across, heaving herself and Eva up over a mound on the other side. Looking around, she saw that they had come out on the other side of the forest and were now in open country. In each direction she could see farmland, fields stretching out for as far as the dim light would allow. On the left, the land rose slowly and about four hundred metres away at the top of the hill she could just pick out the silhouette of black farm buildings. She took off in that direction, still hugging Eva as close to her as possible.

As she got close to the farm, Eszter could see the farmhouse straight in front of her with a barn and farm buildings spread out on each side of it. She lay on her stomach close to a paddock fence, hesitating as she decided what her next step should be. She was sure she could hide overnight in the barn without being disturbed, which would at least give her a few hours in the dry and relative warmth. But she knew that Eva needed cleaning up and more milk. Eszter herself had had nothing to drink since some water about two days ago, and she could not remember when she last had any solid food. She knew she needed something to eat and drink herself if her breast milk for the baby was not to dry up completely. She could see a candle light flickering in the farmhouse window and a thin ribbon of smoke drifting out of the chimney above. She pulled herself to her feet and started to walk slowly towards the farmhouse door. When she reached it, she tapped quietly, almost apologetically.

CHAPTER 4

The farmhouse door was opened a fraction by an elderly woman, who peered suspiciously at them through the open crack, her hand shaking a little on the door handle. Eszter could just see her painfully thin white-haired husband standing nervously like a crane fly a little way behind the woman's right shoulder. The woman stared impassively straight at her, and for a split second Eszter feared she must have made a terrible mistake. At that moment Eva gave a little whimper and, looking down, the woman saw the baby nestling tightly in Eszter's clothing. Without saying a word, the woman very slowly pulled the door open. Eszter realised that they were being invited in.

The farmhouse was sparse inside; the couple were clearly very poor with little in the way of material belongings. But in the middle of the room was the fire which was burning wood and giving some warmth at least in to the room. The woman raised her arm towards a chair in front of the fire, inviting Eszter to approach the fire and sit down. Once Eszter was seated, she handed her a bowl of warm lentil soup and a spoon. 'Thank you,' Eszter said in Hungarian, starting to slowly spoon the soup gratefully into her mouth. When she was finished, the woman took the soup bowl from her and handed her a basin of warm water, a piece of soap and a cloth. Eszter unwrapped the blanket full of faeces and urine from around Eva, testing the water temperature in the basin with her elbow before gently lowering the baby into it and starting to wash her clean. She squeezed the warm water from the cloth over the baby, very gently dabbing the dirt from her body, being especially gentle when washing the raw skin around her groins which had been rubbed sore from days of lying in urine and faeces. As she washed her, the baby looked up at her mother and, for the first time in a long while, gave her a smile. Eszter could not hide her joy, and turned to the old woman, passing the smile back to her in a thank you.

That night Eszter and her baby slept soundly. The woman had led Eszter up some wooden steps to a small room in the attic of the farmhouse. It was barely big enough for the single bed with hessian mattress which it contained, but the room was clean and, above all, dry. Eszter could not remember when she had last had a good night's sleep, and almost as soon as she laid her head down she was unconscious. Her baby Eva was well fed, washed and clean, and likewise did not stir once during the night. Eszter woke the next morning to the sun streaming through the attic window. She fed Eva, got up, dressed, and walked downstairs with the baby in her arms. The fire in the main room had gone out and the old man was nowhere to be seen, but the old lady bid her good morning and offered her a bowl of porridge and a glass of fresh milk.

The two women sat together in the cold living room of the farm house and started to talk to each other. Speaking in German, tentatively at first, especially on the part of the old lady, they got to know each other.

'How long have you lived here in this farm?' Eszter asked the woman.

The old lady started to tell her story.

CHAPTER 5

The old lady told Eszter that she and her husband had previously lived all of their lives in the small Polish village of Brzezinka nearby. She described how in 1941 their village had been cleansed of its inhabitants and then destroyed to build the second concentration camp, Auschwitz II, or Birkenau, as it was then called by its German name. She and her husband had only just managed to flee the place before the village was forcefully evacuated and then destroyed.

By pure luck, her husband Artur had overheard a conversation two German soldiers were having the morning before their village was ransacked. He was delivering milk to a farm nearby where the soldiers were billeted. They were standing in the farmyard smoking together when he arrived with his horse and cart. As he jumped down and started to unload the milk churns from the back of the cart he was close enough to them to hear their conversation. They were discussing the fact that they had been ordered to fall in with their company outside the village of Brzezinka at six o'clock the next morning. There was to be a raid on the village to ransack it and 'cleanse' it of its inhabitants. Once the villagers had all fled or been shot, the houses were to be razed to the ground. A decision had come down from high command that this was to be the site on which a second concentration camp next to Auschwitz was to be constructed and that building work on the new camp was to begin immediately.

So on his way home, Artur started to think quickly. He was passing a small farm, which he had already noticed had been deserted for some time. He stopped off to explore the place. He found that the front door of the farmhouse was not locked and incredibly the key was still on the inside of the door. Inside there was no sign of any recent activity. The place was full of dirt and vermin, with cobwebs hanging from the ceilings. But he found that the water supply was still running and that the farmhouse was dry and secure from the elements. The roof was still in good condition. There was absolutely no sign of anyone having lived there recently, whatever the reason for it having been deserted might be. He removed the key from the inside of the door and locked the place up as he left.

That evening, the husband and wife worked frantically into the night packing as many of their belongings as they could onto their cart. Even so, they had to leave much of what they owned behind. After very little sleep, at four o'clock the next morning, while it was still dark, they left their village for the last time, escaping on their horse and cart before the German army arrived and evacuated the whole village of Brzezinka by force. They heard later that many people were beaten and killed. Most of the houses of the village, including their own, were burnt to the ground and the bulldozers followed very shortly after to clear the remaining structures and debris. They were so lucky to get away in time, having had a chance warning about what was to take place.

Throughout the next day, from the front window of their hastily acquired new home, they could see scores of families, including very young children, the disabled and infirm elderly grandparents fleeing down the road in despair. People were leaving the village where they had lived – as had their families for generations before them – with no idea where they should go. At the main crossroads just down the road they could see families hesitating and then taking a decision whether to head along the road north, west or east. Irena described a scene of confusion and panic, with people shouting and screaming in tears, as those that had been lucky enough to escape fled in fear for their lives.

Artur and Irena started a new life on the farm and, when the German builders and troops arrived in the place where their village had been, no one was to know that they had not been living on this farm nearby all their lives. As luck would have it, the Germans left them alone – they were, it seemed, too busy constructing the new Birkenau camp and getting it ready for its use – and over time they were able to get by on the farm which provided them with enough produce to live on without starving.

After they arrived on the farm they found three or four cows wandering around uncared for in the fields nearby. They assumed these must have been left behind when the farm was abandoned. They brought them into the barn and started to look after them properly. After only a short time the cows were producing more milk than the two of them needed for their own use. One day, they received a visit from the camp adjutant, who asked them if they would supply milk for the soldiers who were being stationed in the camp. Artur had met him on the road and had struck up some sort of acquaintance with the man. He had pretended to show a welcome to the invaders, although, of course, this could not have been farther from the truth about how they really felt. They had no choice. However, they were very lucky that, perhaps because of this, the man took a less aggressive approach towards them. Most of the time the Nazis just took what they needed from farms around them, by violence if necessary, with no chance of payment in return.

From then on, they were able to sell the bulk of the milk their cows produced on a regular basis to the SS guards in the camp nearby. They were not happy at the thought that they were collaborating with the enemy, albeit in this small way, but they had no money and this was the only way they could earn some if they were to survive. Even then, what they were paid for the milk was a paltry sum. And from time to time, if the guard receiving the milk was in a bad mood, or just felt like demeaning him for the sake of highlighting the invaders' superiority, Artur would come away with no milk and no payment for his trouble.

Every morning, after the cows had been milked, Artur would load the churns onto his horse and cart and drive along a track through the woods to the rear gate of the camp. He very soon learnt that the whole compound which had grown up was not just a prison to incarcerate Jews and others who had been arrested, but an extermination camp for the thousands that were being transported into it by train every day. Comments that the camp guards made to him from time to time, once they got to know him, made this clear. But in any case, he had seen in the distance the naked men, women and children being herded in to the gas chambers and had smelt the stench of burning flesh and seen the acrid smoke billowing out of the crematorium chimneys. Their neighbours in the nearby farms also knew exactly what was going on, although they were reticent to talk about it for fear of being arrested and put to death themselves if they were overheard discussing the camp's real purpose. The people around them all bore a sense of profound shame about what was taking place in their Polish motherland, and right there on their doorstep – as did Artur and Irena themselves.

CHAPTER 6

Having heard the old couple's story, Eszter took up the exchange and started to tell the old lady her own story. She told her how she and her family had been arrested by the Gestapo and dragged from their home in Budapest late one night, for the only reason that they were Jewish. They had been denounced by their immediate neighbours, whom they thought were their friends. She described the horror of their transportation to Auschwitz by train in a cattle wagon not long after; and her miraculous escape just metres away from what she had since realised would have been the death of herself and her baby girl; how she and her young baby had hidden in a ditch in the woods during the night, listening at the search which was taking place around them, before escaping through the woods and knocking on the farmhouse door asking for sanctuary.

Any triumph that her story of escape might have contained, however, had just been expunged from her thoughts for Eszter by what the old lady had just confirmed to her about the purpose of the concentration camps. It was corroboration of her worst fears, and Eszter realised that her mother, father, sister and aunt must have entered the sheds with the hundreds of other prisoners who had been ordered from their train and very soon after must all have been gassed to death. She was not able to cry in front of this sympathetic old lady; at this point she just felt completely emotionally dry inside. She knew that the tears would come later and then not cease for the rest of her life. She sat there rocking her baby Eva gently and sadly from side to side.

After a few minutes Eszter looked up at the old woman. 'What are Eva and I going to do?' she asked in desperation.

'I have already discussed this with Artur before he left on the milk delivery this morning,' Irena said to her. 'We think it is best that you stay with us here. It's too dangerous for you to try to escape. You will almost certainly be arrested immediately and sent back to your death in the camp. If you stay here with us here, it is unlikely that you will be found out. If they are looking for you, it is not likely that they would expect you to be hiding so near to the camp from where you have escaped. If asked, we shall say that you are our daughter and that we are looking after you following the birth of your child.'

Eszter could not believe what she was hearing. How could these people be so kind? She felt humbled, after the brutality which she had recently experienced, to come upon such human compassion.

'I don't know how to thank you,' she said to Irena. 'You are offering to save the lives of myself and my little Eva – whom you had never met before last night – and to give us both a future again. You must realise that this could put you and your husband in mortal danger yourselves?'

The old lady sat down next to Eszter and took both her hands in hers. 'We are old people and do not have so long to live. We have had children of our own but they have all been taken from us by this war. We discussed the situation together long after you and Eva had gone to bed last night. We decided your appearance at the door was a sign from God. That it was meant to be, and that it is one small thing that we can do to try and right the shame that has come upon our country.'

'I don't know how I will ever repay you both,' Eszter said, tears filling her eyes.

'We don't expect to be repaid,' Irena replied. 'Giving you and your little baby somewhere safe to live until the war has passed and it is possible for you to return happy and well to your home in Hungary will be all the payment we desire.'

At that moment there was the sound of a horse and cart pulling up outside and the old lady's husband Artur appeared through the door. Eszter ran to him in joy to express her thanks. He put his arm around her shoulder as if she was his own daughter and said nothing, but gave her a broad smile.

CHAPTER 7

July, 1944

Peter stood rigidly to attention in front of his commanding officer, who sat at the desk in front of him. His legs were shaking under him, as was the rest of his body; but his mind was clear. He knew that this was the most serious situation he had ever had to face in his life. He knew that the outcome of this interview was crucial, that perhaps his life depended on it. In spite of the situation, he felt fleetingly surprised that he could feel mentally so calm. 'Many times man lives and dies, between his two eternities' his favourite poet had said. Peter knew this was one of those times.

Almost as soon as the Hungarian young woman had broken out of the line – with his acquiescence – the sirens had started their ear-piercing wail. He looked down at his feet at something that had caught his eye. It was a small white doll made out of corn shreds, lying in the mud next to his right foot. It had obviously fallen out of the blanket the baby was wrapped in. He bent down to pick it up and placed it deep into a pocket of his uniform. Looking up, he saw that the girl was already sprinting over the stony ground, weaving towards the electrified wire fence clutching her baby inside her coat. In a split second she had somehow dragged herself through a loose part of the electrified wire, run across the waste ground the other side and disappeared through the hedge into the woods beyond. She had somehow avoided the hail of machine gun fire that was raining all around her from the lookout turrets. Peter stood there watching the whole episode almost distractedly in slow motion. As the sirens reached their deafening crescendo, he felt searing pain as his right arm was wrenched up forcefully behind him. He knew at once that he was under arrest for letting her go.

'Soldat Leahy,' his commanding officer addressed him directly from across the desk. 'You are here to explain why it was that you allowed one of the prisoners to escape, apparently with your assistance. What have you got to say for yourself?'

'Forgive me, Hauptmann Schön,' Peter said, replying without hesitation. 'I have no excuse. I was very tired. The woman pleaded for a moment to feed her young baby. I allowed her to step to the side to do so. I had no idea that she would break free and disappear through the wire like she did. Please accept my apologies, Sir. This was an error which I had not intended and will never repeat again.'

Hauptmann Schön looked straight at Peter, taking in his fair hair and blue eyes, for what seemed an age, considering his options. Peter stood there immobilised, hoping that the commanding officer had not for any reason guessed his true Polish identity. He also knew enough to be aware that this was not just about himself: the life of his platoon commander as well as his own might have been put in jeopardy by the fact that he had allowed the girl to escape. That in itself could be enough reason for his commanding officer to take the harshest possible approach to Peter in his fear and anger about what this escape might mean for himself. He might be calculating that, if her were to take the severest action against Peter – by having him taken out and summarily shot – this could mitigate any criticisms his superiors might have against him as the SS platoon commander for 'allowing' the escape to happen. The clock on the wall ticked.

'Normally this behaviour would lead to immediate court martial, the outcome of which you are aware, should you be found guilty,' Schön said at last. 'However, you have had no previous black marks against your name, and I cannot see that this aberration has benefitted you in any way.' He paused again.

'I am therefore going to recommend that you shall be reprimanded for failing in your duty to the Führer and the Wehrmacht. You will be demoted from the SS and returned to front line duties, wherever that might take you. Dismissed!'

Without further chance for discussion, Peter was led away by the two guards who had brought him to the hearing and pushed into a cell without ceremony. The door was slammed behind him and the key turned in the lock. The guards marched away and he saw nobody for the rest of the day. He lay on a small hay roll, sleeping only fitfully that night. He had been sentenced and imprisoned without any formal trial, but he was aware that he was indeed lucky not to have been marched straight out and shot. He had no option but to tolerate his incarceration and hope that his luck might change.

* * *

From then on, Peter was left in solitary confinement with no further communication from his commanding officer or anyone else in the camp. He was fed twice a day, but barely enough to keep him alive. Worse than starvation, however, was the fact that he had nobody to talk to and no time on the outside of this cramped and stinking cell. The days turned in to weeks, the weeks dragged on into months. The solitary confinement was unbearable, and he feared that he might eventually lose his mind. He began to wish that they had put an end to him, that they had taken him out and shot him following his trial.

CHAPTER 8

December, 1944

One morning at dawn, without any warning or explanation, Peter awoke to hear the metal footsteps of two of his guards approaching his cell. His cell door was thrown open and he was frog-marched outside. It was the first time he had been out in the open for months and he could hardly see in front of himself, the bright light blinding his vision. In the yard he was bundled onto the back of a truck with twenty or so other prisoners under armed guard. After a long wait the engine of the truck roared into life and the truck started heading out of the camp. He had no idea where they were going, or indeed if this was to be the firing squad at last. He had been offered neither food nor drink before leaving, and when he was unable to suppress the urge to urinate any longer he had no option but to let the urine flow down the legs of his uniform trousers onto his boots and into a puddle on the floor of the lorry around them. He no longer felt any indignity in his position and the other men around him seemed not to notice, or not to care in any case.

Peter drifted in and out of sleep for the whole of that day, as the truck drove slowly and monotonously along what, from the sound of the wheels, were apparently muddy tracks. Eventually, they came to a stop as the light started to fail. The back flap was lowered and the men were ordered off the truck onto the side of the track. Peter jumped down from the truck with the other men, all cautiously looking about them. They were at the edge of a forest. It occurred to Peter at once that, if they had been condemned to face the firing squad, this would be the place for his captors to take them. They were herded together and led under guard towards a clearing about a hundred metres into the trees and away from the road. Peter and the other prisoners stood to attention facing their guards, their faces raised towards them, defiantly awaiting their fate.

After a minute or two the prisoners were ordered to about turn and then marched in line up a small path which took them further into the forest. At the end of this path they arrived at a disused old wooden barn in the middle of a clearing. The door to the barn was thrown open, they were pushed inside and the door then slammed and bolted after them. After about another thirty minutes the door was opened and metal bowls of cold thin soup passed in to them. The door was then bolted again, apparently for the night. Peter and the other men settled down as best they could, finding bales of straw or planks of wood to make some sort of bed to sleep on. The fear they'd had that they were about to be put to death was replaced by the understanding that, whatever their fate was to be, this was to be postponed until the next day at least.

Peter found himself lying on his own in one corner at the back of the barn. By the snoring and movements he could hear around him he knew that the other men had settled to sleep, but he was not able to do the same. He lay there, turning from side to side at intervals, going through the events of the previous few months and his summary demise. He found it hard to believe that, at one moment he had been an apparently valued member of the revered SS Auschwitz camp guard platoon, while at the next he had fallen to ignominious dismissal without any sort of proper trial or appeal of his sentence. He knew that his mere presence in the ranks of the Wehrmacht – let alone his recruitment to the SS camp guard – could never have happened if his true Polish heritage had ever been discovered. The Polish people were considered *untermenschen* by the Germans, as indeed were all Slavic peoples.

At the same time, he felt an overwhelming sense of relief. As a member of the majority rank and file guards – separate from the officers – he had never been sympathetic to the SS and its conduct. He had somehow fallen into the role, having being transferred sideways from the ranks of the Wehrmacht to this posting by default, and certainly not from any ambition on his part. He had not been happy in this life, and since he had arrived in Auschwitz as a member of the SS camp guard, he had become sickened by what was taking place. He was only ever employed in guarding the prisoners as they were brought off the trains at the railhead to Birkenau, but was repulsed by the stories he heard from his colleagues in other platoons about the mass murder that was going on within the camp. Most of his fellow guards seemed to relish the situation and enjoy the task in hand, beating and murdering prisoners as they went. They even bragged openly about their conduct. He found it difficult to believe, however, that there were no other members of his platoon who were as unhappy in this posting as he was and were as reluctant participants in their duties as he had been. In some ways he felt that whatever was to come next – even transfer to the Russian front, perhaps – could not be more degrading than the death camp he had been expected to be a guard of and had since been evicted from.

Peter lay there on his own, not sleeping but unable to discuss his thoughts with any of those close to him. He looked around in the dim light of the barn. He had no idea where they were, but calculated from the ponderous progress the truck had made and the time he had been on it that they were probably still in Poland. He had no idea where they might be heading: if not to their deaths by firing squad in the forest the next morning or, worse, on the front line, then how long might he still have to live? In spite of the uncertainty about what lay ahead for him, however, his banishment from his post in Auschwitz had resulted in a yoke being lifted from around his neck.

As he lay there mulling over all these issues, Peter had a sense that there was some light coming in somewhere from the outside. It was probably too early for dawn, but perhaps the light was from the moon? As this glimmer of light in the barn increased, he saw that there was a corner of the wooden wall next to where he was lying that was allowing light to enter through a crack. He reached out his left hand and pushed gently at one of the wooden slats of the wall, the one closest to the ground. As soon as he touched the wood, he realised that it was wet and completely rotten. He eased himself up on his left elbow and reached over with his right arm to apply more pressure on the board. Gently, and miraculously noiselessly, he was able to prise the board apart. The rotten wood came away in pieces in his hand and he started to lever the board above it quietly to and fro. In a few minutes he was able to lever this rotten piece free as well.

After about fifteen minutes, Peter had freed a narrow gap in the corner of the barn wall. He moved nearer towards it on his elbows and, after removing one or two more rotten slats, he had made a gap wide enough for him to crawl very slowly through on his stomach. Once he was completely through, he turned round and, as quietly as he could, replaced the larger pieces of board that were still intact over the hole he had made, to conceal the window of light from entering the barn as best he could.

Peter lay flat, face down on the ground outside the barn, his heart pumping loudly in his chest. He was out of the prison he had been thrown in to, but nowhere near freedom. After some more minutes lying still, he knew that he had no option but to continue his escape. He knew that he not only had to get free of the camp and the soldiers that must be sleeping around it – and probably guarding it – but also away from the area completely if his escape was to be achieved. Now that he was out of the barn he could see that the light which had come to his aid was indeed provided by a full moon shining through the tops of the trees. This would make his escape more risky, but he had to take his chance. He could also see that the forest was no more than about twenty metres across the clearing from where he was lying. Above the silhouette of the trees, in the opposite direction from the full moon, was the faint beginning of the light of dawn appearing in the sky. He had no time to lose. He had to complete his escape now if he was going to get free. He knew that failure and re-capture would mean almost certain death from a bullet in the back as he ran, or in his heart as he stood tied to a post in front of a firing line.

Peter raised himself up to a crouching position and very quietly but smoothly crept towards the line of trees. He did not stop to look behind to see if there were any guards watching him. He knew he just had to keep moving once he had started. As soon as he reached the cover of the first trees, he increased his pace, still stooping low, but now running from his captivity. The undergrowth was mossy and soggy, which made the going difficult, but had the advantage that there was less likelihood of dry wooden branches on the ground which might crack under foot and give him away. After he was about fifty metres into the forest, he stood completely upright and started running for his life.

Once he had reached the other side of the forest area, where the trees started to thin out, he had to make his next decision. Looking out through the trees, it appeared that there was only farmland in the distance as far as he could see. He found himself next to a large, dead half-hollowed tree and decided by instinct to cram himself as much as he could into the protection of this. The hollowed side was facing towards the farmland, and he was therefore obscured from anyone who might be following him out through the forest. He lay upright in that position in the hollow tree as the sun rose, listening for the shouts and shots from his pursuers which he expected to hear at any moment.

As the day wore on, however, no such noise reached him. He continued to lie upright, without moving, in the hollow of the tree, his body numbed by this position and the circulation in his legs feeling as if it had ceased. By what must have been afternoon, he eventually came to the conclusion that he was not being hunted. Thinking about it, it occurred to him that perhaps he had not even been missed. He had not noticed any sort of head count, let alone a roll call, that had been made when the truck stopped for the night. It seemed more and more likely that the guards had woken up, loaded the men back onto the truck and driven on again without noticing his absence or the hole in the corner of the wall at the back of the barn. He knew he still had to be extremely careful, but the more time passed he gradually felt able to relax. He shook his right leg, which had gone completely numb, out of the tree hollow and then his left leg. Cautiously, he stood outside his natural hiding place and looked around at the farmland around him. He then stepped back into the cover of the forest, found a more comfortable place to lie down next to a fallen tree trunk, and waited some more.

CHAPTER 9

Dusk had arrived, and Peter knew that it would soon be time for him to move on under the cover of night. The bright full moon from the night before had given way to a very slight sliver of a new moon. He thanked his luck for this. Once it was completely dark, he started to walk across the fields in front of him, ignoring any roads that might be nearby. His training had taught him to navigate roughly by the stars at night, and he plotted a course that would take him approximately due south. His SS uniform had been torn from his back when he had been returned to the cell following his summary dismissal by Hauptmann Schön, but he still had on the regulation Wehrmacht shirt, trousers and boots that he'd been left with which would give him away. He knew he had to exchange these as soon as possible for something less incriminating.

He reached the end of a large field and peered over the hedge at the crossroad in front of him. There was only one signpost still standing, but he could see from this that he was still in southern Poland. Incredibly, he was perhaps still only about fifty kilometres from Auschwitz, where he had come from. And therefore about the same distance from the village of Brzezinka where his parents had been living when he last saw them. His initial instinct was to turn around and head as far away from the place as he could, perhaps north towards Łodz or Warsaw. But he thought it best to avoid heading for any centres of population, let alone big cities. And in any case, wherever he travelled in Poland he would now be in German occupied territory. As he stood there pondering his options, his head told him that to track back towards the place from where he had come was not such a ridiculous idea. If his escape from the barn had been noted, then searches would continue in ever widening circles from that place, and from there eventually to the Polish border itself. If he had not been missed, then there was even less likelihood that he would be apprehended near the place he had previously been stationed.

Before long, after traipsing over field after field to keep his route away from roads, Peter came to a small hamlet. He crept along behind the few scattered houses and came across the back yard of one of them. Hanging on a washing line there were a number of items of a man's clothing. He looked around him. There was no one in sight. He jumped the stone wall, reached up and clutched some of the pieces of clothes with one hand, and jumped back over the wall again. He crouched down and inspected his catch. There were two old shirts, a pair of socks and a farmer's breeches. These would have to do. He felt guilty about stealing from a Polish farmer who probably had only very few clothes to his name, but knew he had no choice. He put the clothes on and stuffed the Wehrmacht shirt and trousers into an old linen bag he had picked up from the ground next to the clothesline. He would dispose of these as soon as he could, but somewhere as far away from human traffic as possible. A ditch covered with undergrowth would be a good idea.

Leaving the hamlet behind, Peter jumped over fences and started to trudge through fields, heading roughly south, as far as he could determine. He made a point of creeping round the perimeter of each field, keeping low and as near to the hedges and walls as he could. He figured that he was less likely to be detected in this way. He would have made much quicker progress were he to stride across the middle of one field after another, but knew that would carry much more of a risk of him being seen and apprehended.

After about an hour trudging through fields, occasionally having to scurry across a farm track between one field and another, he came to the edge of a narrow road. As he navigated along the hedge next to the road he could see through gaps over the hedge that the road opened up in front of him and joined two larger roads at a crossroad. In the dark he could see the silhouette of an army truck parked there and hear men's voices. He came to an immediate halt, crouched down low and waited, giving himself time to assess the situation.

Crouching still for five minutes or so, he heard the sound of rifle butts thudding on the metal road and men talking German. He guessed he had stumbled on an army checkpoint stationed at the crossroads. He was unable to see how many soldiers there were there, but assumed there were more than he would be able, unarmed, to overpower, were he to come into a fight with them. He didn't have to decide on his next move, however, because at that moment the engine of the truck roared into action; the grey silhouette of the truck started to move down the road to where he was hiding and its headlights swung directly towards him.

Peter froze. He had fallen flat on his face the moment the engine of the truck came to life, and all he could do now was to lie rigid on his stomach in the corner of the field. Luckily he had dumped the linen bag with his discarded bits of Wehrmacht uniform in a ditch an hour or so back. It flashed through his mind that if he were to be apprehended, he did not have any identity on him, but he hoped he may be able to bluff it out and pass himself off as a local Polish farm hand if this was to happen. The headlights of the truck soared past him, not so far above his head, and the vehicle disappeared up the road and away from him. He took a deep breath and relaxed, but did not move for another ten minutes or so. He realised that it was by pure luck that he had seen the truck before the soldiers saw him. He continued on his way across the fields, but now with even more care than before.

CHAPTER 10

December, 1944

Arno Claussen was walking along the riverside, returning to his office in Paulay Ede Street. It was nearly dark. As he got near to the Hungarian Parliament building he saw three trucks pulling up along the road by the riverbank just in front of him. He saw half a dozen militiamen with rifles jump out of each truck. In the dim light he could just make out their uniforms of the fascist Arrow Cross militia. He sensed they were up to no good. He was only about fifty metres away and stopped behind the broad trunk of a large tree, to observe what was going on without being seen.

The rear of the first truck was flung open and scores of men, women and children jumped and fell out of the back of the truck. There were shouts in defiance from some of the men and a rising wail of crying from the women and children. Claussen saw that they all had the yellow Star of David attached to their chests. He guessed they had been brought here from the Budapest ghetto. He knew from his contacts that there were reported to be up to seventy thousand Jewish men, women and children incarcerated in the ghetto since it was first established at the end of November, and he'd heard that many more were being rounded up and thrown in there every day that passed. As soon as the Nazis entered Budapest they had started to raid Jewish homes, under orders from Adolf Eichmann. Those that refused go into the ghetto were beaten up and dragged out to be shot.

He and his colleagues had been attempting to find a way of making contact with those inside the ghetto. But this was proving very difficult. The area where the ghetto had been established, which consisted of several blocks of the old Jewish quarter of the city including the two main synagogues, was surrounded by a high fence and stone wall that was guarded at all times to stop people getting in or out. It was completely cut off from the outside world; none of his friends had been able to gain access to the inside of the ghetto or get news into those people they knew who were incarcerated within it. There was also no way of getting food or other help to the families inside. They had heard a rumour that there was an epidemic of typhoid raging through the inhabitants.

He had no idea where this information had come from, but it didn't surprise him.

From where he stood behind a tree, Arno could see that the poor people were being pulled roughly away from the truck and forced forward by a line of militiamen standing each side of the truck. They were being beaten with rifle butts and smacked around their faces with rifle barrels to force them away from the truck towards the riverbank. There they were spread out in a line along the side of the river facing the water and ordered to take off their shoes. Men and boys, women and girls were all bending down to remove their shoes as ordered. Mothers were removing their own shoes before ripping the tiny shoes off their babies' feet and flinging them onto the ground after them. Looking over the parapet near to where he was standing, Claussen could see that the river was at high tide, in full flood with the current carrying it rapidly southwards out of the city.

There was a deathly pause. With no warning, a volley of shots rang out from the militiamen who had lined up behind the prisoners. Claussen saw the men, women and children falling forwards in slow motion, like leaves in the autumn wind, falling to their deaths. Most of the victims fell directly into the river and were rapidly consumed by the raging torrent of water which carried them away. Once the shooting ceased, the militiamen walked along the line of those bodies that were still lying on the water's edge, ramming their rifle butts into the heads of the victims who were not yet dead – they had clearly been ordered not to waste bullets unnecessarily – and heaving all of the bodies that remained on the riverbank into the water. These too went to join the many others who were being borne away by the fast flowing waters, free at last from their pain and suffering forever.

A minute or two passed, while the Arrow Cross men cleared the river bank of bodies, leaving the shoes on the ground where the murdered prisoners had fallen. They made no attempt to conceal the blood on the ground. As soon as the task was completed, the men turned and headed for the next truck, throwing the back open, and as before violently heaving the men, women and children out, lining them up facing the river, ordering them to discard their shoes and shooting them in the back as they stood awaiting their fate.

Claussen could not bear to watch the massacre that was taking place in front of him, but he knew he could not move away from his place of concealment. If any of the soldiers were to notice him walking away, he had no doubt that he too would be apprehended and added to the firing line. He was also aware of the fact that he was a lone witness to this act of inhumanity, the only person there that night who might be called upon to give evidence in the future about the genocide that was being carried out. He knew that he had to survive to tell the world about what had taken place here on the banks of the Danube this night, not only for his own sake but for those that were being slaughtered. He had a duty not to be discovered watching the killing events. He therefore stood absolutely still where he was, as one truck after the other was emptied of its human cargo and the men, women and children within it summarily executed.

The last truck was emptied and the last group of innocent families murdered. The militiamen shut up the backs of the trucks, jumped back in and, one by one, the trucks pulled away and out of the area. Claussen had no doubt that they would return with more innocent victims from the ghetto, if not that night then on succeeding nights until they exhausted their death quota or the ghetto was empty of human life. He waited for a while, to be certain that he was alone, and then stood out from where he had been concealed behind the tree.

He walked to the water's edge and looked down. Not a single body remained on the riverbank; the soldiers had seen to that. The human remains were being swept down to their watery graves, wherever the river chose to carry them. Scattered around on the muddy ground were pieces of clothing which had fallen, children's dolls and other items that people had dropped on the ground where they stood. Grim evidence of the atrocity he had just witnessed. The grimmest evidence of all was the line of dozens of items of footwear – men's and women's shoes of all types, clogs and boots and the shoes of children of all ages including the tiny booties of babies. Claussen stood looking down at this pitiful display and wept.

CHAPTER 11

Claussen was standing on the pavement at the end of his street. He was pressed into the entrance to a small shop, which was closed. It was well after midnight. It was also freezing cold and he had been positioned there, without moving, for nearly three hours now. He was beginning to despair that there would not be any activity that night, that something must have gone seriously wrong.

Suddenly, Claussen heard a whistle. He waited the prescribed ten seconds and the whistle came again. He whistled back twice, in quick succession. He broke his cover and turned into the entrance to an alleyway which passed down the side of the building, linking Paulay Ede Street with Andrassy Avenue. He stood there still, pressed closely against the wall, waiting for movement. Very slowly one, then two, three and four silhouettes appeared at the far end of the alley, creeping furtively towards where he stood. As the first person reached him Claussen grabbed him by the sleeve without a word, but squeezed his elbow to reassure the man by this contact that he was in the right place but should remain silent. As they stood together not speaking, Claussen saw the other silhouetted figures approaching. Behind the man were a woman and a youth holding the hands of two small children. As he looked back up the alleyway he saw another silhouette, that of the contact who had delivered them into his safe keeping, turn and disappear out of sight. Claussen waited until they were all assembled together and formed them silently into a single file, pushing them hard up against the wall.

With a brief wave of his hand, Claussen lead the way and beckoned the group to follow him in single file. Slowly and silently he crept back along the alley and stopped at the corner where it turned into Paulay Ede Street. Claussen stopped and listened, not ready to proceed until he had convinced himself as much as he could that the coast was clear. When he had finally done so, he gave another brief wave and led the group out of the alley along the side of his street. Number sixteen was only a matter of metres away. As he reached his house, the door opened for him and Claussen stood back away just a little, ushering the people inside, one by one. When they had all disappeared silently inside, he continued to stand outside the door for a few more moments, looking and listening carefully up and down the street in both directions. He heard not a single sound and, reassured, turned and followed the group into his house, shutting the door quietly behind him. His wife Hanneke was standing by the door and gave him a silent hug. She had already shown the group through the door at the back of his office into their family apartment.

Only when he entered their living room was Claussen able to see the group of people he had taken in. There was a mother and father and two young children as well as the youth who was presumably an older son. He didn't ask questions. They were standing together looking straight at him, undisguised fear on all their faces. The woman carried a small cardboard suitcase in her hand. Each one of them had the yellow Star of David stitched to the breast of their jacket, with the word 'Jude' written on it. The man stepped forward and stretched out his hand in thanks, bowing slightly to Arno as he did so. Claussen shook the proffered hand firmly in acceptance. Hanneke beckoned to the family to take a seat at the table and started to hand round bowls of meat soup. Nobody spoke. They were all still too frightened to start a conversation. But they started to eat the soup with ravenous haste, as people who are starving do.

Arno Claussen was now working with his friend Raoul Wallenberg, helping him and the others in his group with his urgent plan to find safe houses for as many of the Jews threatened with murder as they possibly could. Thousands of Jews were being murdered every day by the Nazis, being shot in the street or transported out of the city to the extermination camps in Poland, the news of the operation of which had filtered down to Wallenberg and his contacts. Wallenberg was the Swedish special envoy in Budapest, and one of Arno's Jewish lawyer friends had introduced Arno to him as someone who would be prepared to help their cause. Wallenberg had been issuing protective passports to as many Jewish people as he could and sheltering Jewish families in buildings which he designated as 'Swedish territory'. Arno and his wife were just two of scores of like-minded people doing whatever they could to save these people. Each time Arno was able to provide a temporary safe haven for another group of Jews, he said a prayer and asked divine providence that this group should not be the last.

Once they had finished eating what was probably the first meal they had had in days, Arno and Hanneke showed their guests to their hiding place. This was in a small space that Arno had constructed in the wall behind the wardrobe in Arno and Hanneke's own bedroom. By making a false wall in front of the existing wall he had created a secret space which was only just large enough for three adults and a couple of children to squeeze into. He had placed a small door, which was no bigger than a hatch, as the entrance to the hiding place. The door was hidden by the wardrobe when it was moved back into its place. Inside the hideout, there was not enough room for a bed, but the space was just enough for the fugitives to lie head to foot on the blankets that Hanneke had placed on the floor. She had left some water bottles and a few pieces of bread there for them, as well as a supply of books for the occupants to read while they hid, although all they had for light was a handful of candles. To use the Claussen's toilet and bathroom the family had to wait for a time when there was nobody else with him in the office – in case clients visiting him were to overhear people moving around in the apartment – and only when Arno and Hanneke could also be sure that the coast was clear on the road outside would they let the visitors out to relieve themselves. With luck, this group would be passed on to another helper the next night and then perhaps safely out of the city to a safe house in the country.

CHAPTER 12

January, 1945

Eszter sat on the river bank with baby Eva in her arms. For the first time in months she felt truly happy. The low winter sunshine was surprisingly warm, rising over the trees on the opposite side of the river in front of her. The riparian forests cast shadows along both banks of the River Vistula. The forest in front of her was full of birch trees, from which the place that was Brzezinka (now called Birkenau in German) had got its name. The thin-leaved deciduous trees had shed their golden leaves in the autumn, as they did every year. Now the denuded trunks with their papery scrolls of bark in colours ranging from snow white to cinnamon brown were standing nakedly before her. Artur had taught her that the birch symbolises growth, renewal, stability, initiation and adaptability; and looking at the trees in this tranquil setting she could not but hope that they somehow represented a totem for the future for herself and her baby Eva.

Through the now bare branches of the thin line of trees in front of her, Eszter could see the flat marshy meadow wastelands of the Vistula valley stretching away for miles. She smiled down at Eva and the baby gave her a lovely smile back. Eva was thriving now, the fresh farm milk, eggs and vegetables that Irena was feeding Eszter had increased her mother's milk, as a result of which she could see that Eva was putting on weight and growing fast. Ever since her birth eight months ago in their Budapest apartment, Eszter had feared constantly that she might lose her child from dehydration, starvation or, worse, by a violent death in front of her. She knew that they both were by no means out of danger from discovery, but for the moment she was content to live for each day and enjoy their life as it was.

Artur and Irena had been so kind to them. They were desperately poor themselves, but did not hesitate to share what they had with Eszter and her baby. In return, they asked for nothing. Eszter did as much as she could to contribute, helping Irena with the cleaning and housework and, now that she was stronger, starting to help Artur outside by hoeing the vegetable garden, collecting the eggs and feeding the hens every morning. The chance to repay these two old people for their kindness by working on the farm and in the house, not to mention the peace and fresh air she was benefitting from, was a joy for Eszter after all the fear and brutality that she and baby Eva had had to endure.

As she sat there feeling happy, Eszter gathered together the pieces of corn she had picked off the floor of the barn that morning. She chose the widest strand she could find and pressed it flat. She then folded it in half and wound it into a figure of eight, the top loop representing a head, the lower half was to become the body. She wound other smaller strands of corn carefully around the waist and then pulled others through them to make a skirt around the bottom half of the body. She had taken to making these corn dolls for baby Eva since shortly after she was born. She had nothing else to give her child as a toy, and made the baby these as her own special dolls to play with and amuse her. Often they would end up being chewed on and destroyed, but as soon as one doll was discarded, Eszter would replace it with another. It only took her a few minutes to make each doll and with practice she was getting more and more expert at making them.

The evening before, Eszter had stood next to Irena in the small farmhouse kitchen, taking each plate from her as she washed and rinsed them, drying each carefully with a cloth.

'It's so good to have my own daughter at last!' Irena smiled at Eszter. 'Artur and I had three sons, but always hoped for a daughter as well. Now we have one!'

'What happened to your sons?' Eszter asked, not wishing to intrude, but sensing that Irena wanted to talk.

'Our three boys enlisted into the Polish army together, and left to defend the border from the threatened German invasion. When the Germans invaded on the first of September 1939, the Polish army's resistance was overwhelmed. The boys and the rest of the Polish army guarding the border had fought gallantly, but it was useless against the power of the invading German army. After being captured they were rounded up by the Nazis with all the other young men in their battalion, probably to be taken away and shot. But the boys managed to negotiate their survival. As it happens, my husband Artur is German by birth from his father, although he and all his family have always lived in Poland and considered themselves Polish. But because of their father's birth our three sons had German as well as Polish citizenship. We later learnt from a neighbour's boy who also escaped that our sons had explained to the Nazis that they were, in fact, German. As a result of this, and no doubt helped by their fair hair and blue eyes, they were released from arrest. But they were then forced to enlist together immediately into the German army. They had no choice and were not able to object for fear of being shot as Polish sympathisers. That was over three years ago, and we've heard nothing from any of them since.'

Once Irena had shared this information with Eszter, a day did not go by when she or Artur spoke about one or other of their sons, telling Eszter family stories and relating the good times they'd had together. They were so proud of their boys, who would never leave their hearts. They feared that they may never set eyes on them again. Irena told Eszter she worried that it was possible that their sons had been sent straight to the Russian front. She had heard bits of gossip from neighbours that all was not well with this campaign and that many men were being lost.

'Jan and Marek were twenty two and twenty three when they enlisted. They were born closely together. As the oldest, Marek was the leader and kept his brothers in order. The two younger boys looked up to him. He was their hero. Jan was a studious boy, always reading books and interested in learning. Artur and I were sure he would have grown up to be a school teacher, or something similar. Peter, the youngest, was eighteen. The baby of the family. He was a romantic, more interested in reading poetry and making up stories. He took great pleasure in teasing his mother at every opportunity, and enjoyed life to the limit.'

Eszter smiled, happy to hear Irena's stories about her sons – which she knew Irena took pleasure in telling her – but she was sad to think that the elderly couple might very well never see their three sons again. She could not help but notice that Irena referred to her boys in the past tense, although she was not aware that she was doing so.

For her part, Eszter told Irena and Artur her own story and her fears for her husband.

'Robert and I met early in 1943 in Budapest and married in May that year. In September he was rounded up together with other Hungarian Jewish men in our district and taken away for 'labour service'. I never saw him again after that, but we heard rumours from other people that the Hungarian Jewish men were actually being used as forced labour in mine quarries and often taken out of the country to work in occupied Ukraine. We never heard from our neighbours and friends about any man who had survived this enforced labour and had subsequently returned to their homes.'

Eszter paused. 'We only had a short time together as man and wife. When I think about him in my loneliness during the day, I feel that I never really had time to get to know him and fear I am already even forgetting what he looks like. I wake up every night in a panic that I am forgetting who my husband is and have nightmares about the suffering he must be going through if he has been captured. I have recurring vivid dreams of his death at the hands of the Nazis. If he is still alive, he has no knowledge of my pregnancy and of Eva's birth.'

Irena and Artur sat quietly listening to Eszter's story and, as they heard what she too had been through, tears welled up in their eyes as much as they had done when they told her about the loss of their own sons.

CHAPTER 13

February, 1945

Eszter was sitting in front of the wood fire with Artur and Irena, as she did every evening. Irena sat next to her, mending Artur's socks and shirts, pulling the almost threadbare material over an antique wooden mending ball as she did so. Baby Eva slept soundly nearby in the makeshift cot Artur had made for her out of slats of wood. Eszter and her baby had been living at the farm for nearly seven months now. At the end of January 1945 the Russian army had invaded Poland. There was war and fighting all around them. Artur had heard news that Soviet forces had now reached the Auschwitz concentration camps a short distance away from them. In advance of the Soviet invasion the Nazis had taken most of the prisoners from the camps and were forcing them westwards in a 'death march'. He had heard that thousands of the prisoners had already perished before they had marched only a short distance from the camp. When they arrived at the camps, the Soviets liberated what remaining prisoners there were still alive left there.

Through the slats in their shuttered windows Artur and Irena had watched hundreds of starving men and women being marched along the road which passed the bottom of the track up to their farm as they were being driven west into Germany in front of the Soviet advancement. Eva sat at the back of the room cuddling baby Eva; she could not bear to watch what was happening right on their doorstep. When Artur ventured out to speak to their neighbours, he brought back with him the news that there was chaos across the countryside of Upper Silesia. Within the space of a few days, the invading Soviet and Ukrainian troops continued to march on relentlessly westwards, forcing a path through the retreating German armies and their prisoners from the camps as they went.

'I think it is time for me and Eva to return to Budapest' Eszter said to her friends. Artur and Irena looked at each other. Irena got up and crouched next to Eszter, holding both of her hands in hers.

'It would be very dangerous to travel in the present conditions, Eva,' she said in a whisper. 'Don't you think you should remain here for a few months more until the situation improves?'

Eszter squeezed Irena's hands gently. 'I understand your concerns,' she said. 'But I think that travelling in this chaos might be better than waiting for things to settle. We have no way of knowing how difficult it might become to travel at all, once the Soviets have tightened their grip on the country, the barriers are erected and the borders fully secured. In any case, we shall be travelling due south, when all the armies and refugees seem to be heading west. You and Artur have been so kind to me and Eva. We will remember you both for always,' she concluded.

So the next morning Artur brought his horse and cart round to the front of the farmhouse, swung Eszter's small bundle of belongings into the back and helped her up on to the seat next to him, before passing little Eva up into her arms. Eszter was determined not to cry, but felt waves of gratitude and affection towards the elderly couple who had given sanctuary to herself and her baby. Artur flicked his whip and clucked his tongue and the cart started to move off.

'Goodbye, Irena! Goodbye!' Eszter called out as she turned to give a final brave wave to Irena and blew her a kiss.

'Goodbye, Eszter! Goodbye, Eva! Stay safe!!' Irena called back, waving at them all the way until the cart reached the road and turned left and out of view.

CHAPTER 14

Eszter had decided to try and make her way back to Budapest by road. She knew that to do so would take much longer than by rail, but that it would be less risky than chancing a railway journey. In any case, she thought that it was likely that the railway network would not be working – for civilians at least – during this period of Russian invasion. In addition to these purely practical calculations, something else inside her repulsed her. She still didn't feel ready to get back on a train; the memory of the recent train journey which had brought her to this place from her home in Hungary had still not left her thoughts and nightmare dreams. The distance she would have to travel by road was about 500km, she calculated, more or less due south. From what she had learnt, the mass of bodies were heading west: German armies and civilians fleeing westwards back into Germany; prisoners from the concentration camps and others being forced to follow them on what was to become to be known as 'The Great March'. And the Russian and Ukrainian armies were following them.

Artur drove them in his cart about ten kilometres south to the small town of Rajsko, stopping at the entrance to a farm on the outskirts which belonged to another farmer whom he knew quite well and trusted. Artur reined in his horse, jumped off the cart and went looking for old man Jakub. He returned with the farmer within only a few minutes. It was clear to Eszter that Jakub had agreed to help immediately. He doffed his cap at Eszter, went back into his barn and emerged again very quickly with his horse and cart. He helped Eszter and baby Eva onto the seat of the cart and threw their small bag of belongings behind them. Without stopping, they waved goodbye to Artur and continued southwards to the Czechoslovakian border. They were stopped many times at Soviet check points, Jakub's cart always searched to make sure he was not concealing arms, but the soldiers were largely uninterested in the mother and her baby, apparently assuming she was Jakub's daughter. At the Czech border there were long queues of people waiting to cross. Jakub helped them both down, unloaded Eszter's bag and wished them all the best. After he had left them there, all Eszter could do was to wait in line for hours with the other refugees who were waiting to cross the border. She was so tired, she repeatedly found herself falling asleep on her feet, only to be pushed in the back by one of the men behind her when the line started to creep forward again.

The journey south across Czechoslovakia was harrowing. Men, women and children were fleeing in their thousands from the oncoming Soviet armies, but again most of them seemed to be moving westwards. After about five hours Eszter managed to get a lift in a van from a baker who was delivering bread to the next town. When she asked during the journey whether it was not difficult for him to continue his trade during this war, he gave her a shrug and a smile. From there it was a question of waiting for lifts when they could get them, mostly a few kilometres at a time but on one occasion with a priest in a battered old car who took them about fifty kilometres. He told Eszter he was going to conduct a family funeral for some old friends of his who had been killed in the recent fighting.

Eszter was careful not to try to strike up acquaintance or to ask too many questions with the people who were kind enough to help them with a lift. But she was always polite and very grateful for the assistance which they were giving. All of the routes which they took were on minor roads or farm tracks, avoiding any sizeable towns or villages. There was evidence of war and destruction all around them: the people she met, some of whom took her and her baby into their dwelling for shelter overnight, were hungry and frightened about the possibility that further conflict and war would bring to their families and their communities.

After eight days of perilous travel, Eszter was sitting on the back of a milk wagon singing a Hungarian lullaby quietly to baby Eva. The rain had stopped. As the farmer climbed down to lift two milk churns off the back of the wagon she asked him where they were.

'How far is it to the Hungarian border now?' she asked the man.

'Only about two kilometres away, over that ridge there,' he said, pointing in the direction of the track they had been following.

Eszter was excited to learn that at last they were not far from her motherland. The farmer said goodbye to the mother and baby just before they finally reached the border at the Danube bridge, and wished them well. After only a short wait Eszter managed to jump onto a truck which was leaving to cross over the bridge to the town of Esztergom, on the Hungarian side of the Danube bend. The border was heavily guarded by Soviet troops and they had to wait hours to be allowed through. Eszter still had her Hungarian identity card in her possession, and she grasped it tightly in her hand now. It was dirty and torn, but at least her name, date of birth and Budapest address was still legible. The photograph was faded and showed a much younger girl, but it was recognisable as a picture of herself. She had kept the precious document, folded into a very small square, inside a fold in the lining of her underpants, ever since she was on the truck as it pulled away from their apartment after she and her family had been arrested by the Gestapo. For the first time since then, she now slid it out from its hiding place as she waited in line and smoothed out the single sheet of paper as best as she could. When her turn finally came, she handed it to the Soviet soldier as nonchalantly as she could. He looked it over, looking bored, and then handed it back to her. He clearly did not expect her to have an identity document for her small baby and did not ask for one. He waved them away. They were free to cross.

By the time they reached Esztergom on the Hungarian side of the river Danube it was nearing nightfall. Eszter got off the truck with Eva in her arms and started walking down the main street of the small town. She walked towards a bar that still had its lights on. Through the front window she could see that there were a number of men, locals and Russian soldiers, seated drinking beer at the tables inside. She walked towards the entrance. The door to the bar was wide open. As she reached the threshold a burly man appeared at the door to see who was there. He stood in front of her, barring her entry. He took just one look at the mother and baby. 'We're closed!' he growled, spitting on the floor and slammed the door in her face.

Eszter walked further on down the street. She came to an old cottage set back a little from the road, opened the iron gate and walked up the path to the low oak door. She knocked politely. An old lady opened the door and stood glaring at Eszter and her baby, looking over steel-rimmed spectacles. 'No gypsies here!' she cried at Eszter, slamming the door in her face even harder than the pub owner had done a few minutes before.

Eszter walked away with tears in her eyes. She was exhausted and miserable. It was clear that she was not going to be offered anywhere to stay in this unfriendly place.

She walked up the hill towards the basilica that stood high above the town of Esztergom, towering over everyone and everything below it. In the dim light its dark silhouette seemed to Eszter more of a threatening rather than a reassuring presence. She entered the basilica grounds nervously and tried the handle of the front door of the church. It was locked. Walking round to the back of the basilica, she came across a small wooden shack. This at least was not locked. She entered the shack, which contained a lot of gardening junk, and lay down on the bare wooden floor with her baby, exhausted and demoralised. She made a makeshift bed from a few pieces of old carpet and some straw and lay down on them with Eva in her arms. She felt very sad at having arrived back in Hungary to such an unwelcoming town. But she was exhausted, and fell asleep at once.

In the morning Eszter rose early but felt better after a sound night's sleep. She fed little Eva and then made her way out of the shack. Outside, the sun was shining and she drank from a water fountain in the basilica grounds. The ice cold water was refreshing as she rubbed it over her face and neck. As she made her way with her baby to the town's jetty there were few people around at this early hour. There were a number of tired-looking soldiers guarding the boats and barges carrying military and industrial equipment which were moored there, but they ignored the young woman with her baby. She sat on the side of the jetty, waiting patiently.

Slowly the town started to wake up and men came and went to the boats. She started to beg for lifts down river. After a couple of hours, she persuaded a man on a wood carrying barge to take them on board. It turned out that he was making for a destination south of Budapest and could take her all the way there. He was a friendly, elderly Hungarian with large whiskers. 'You're sure you want to take the risk, my dear?' he asked her, as if he was her own father. 'You do know there has been fierce fighting for weeks in Budapest and that we shall be entering a war zone? The Soviet armies have finally taken Budapest from the Germans, after two months of fighting.'

Eszter was not aware of any of this, but thanked him for kindly offering to take her, indeed to look after her. 'I understand,' she said to the fatherly figure. 'But I am desperate to get back to my family home, and I trust you.' The man smiled kindly at her, throwing the mooring rope on to the river bank as he manoeuvred the barge slowly out into the centre of the river. Eszter and Eva settled down on a seat at the rear of the barge to watch as the barge made its way slowly down stream.

CHAPTER 15

The barge navigated its way southwards from the Danube bend at Esztergom. It was boarded a number of times by Soviet soldiers who sped out in small boats to apprehend them. They were pulled up at the towns of Visegrad and Vac, where the barge and its contents were searched in detail – the soldiers were apparently looking for arms hidden under the consignment of wood. Each time, practically the whole cargo of wood was unloaded onto the bank, leaving the barge man in despair, having to heave it all back onto the barge again on his own after the search. Each time, Eszter's identity card was examined yet again. But she told the soldiers that she was visiting relatives in Budapest (which she wished silently could be the case), and her Hungarian identity was all in order.

'It's true,' the bargee confided in her as the barge passed the final bend in the river before they saw the city of Budapest ahead of them. 'There are a lot of supplies smuggled down to Budapest by this way, on barges. And not just guns and ammunition, but supplies of all kinds for the black market. Most people know about this. But they and the soldiers also know that nearly all of this takes place at night; in the black moonless nights and, better still, when there is a thick fog. This doesn't stop them searching every barge that comes down in daylight as if they were looking for a needle in a haystack, of course,' he added as if to sign off on his frustration. This was the most he had spoken to her during the whole of their journey down the Danube bend from Esztergom. Eszter did not know what to say in reply, but smiled at him tiredly.

As they passed Margit Island and arrived at that part of the river which flowed through the centre of Budapest, Eszter could not believe what she was seeing. All of the bridges crossing the river, the vital links between the flat area of Pest on her left and the castle hill of Buda on the right, had been blown up by the German army a few weeks before, in a desperate attempt to resist the invading Soviet army. But even more shocking for her to see was the fact that her city of Budapest itself lay in ruins, most of its buildings destroyed or damaged by the street fighting which had occurred in the two months since the end of December. The Soviet forces had encircled Budapest, putting the city under siege, the Red Army and Romanian armies trapping the German and Hungarian armies within the city.

The barge docked briefly at a jetty near to the Parliament building in the centre of Budapest, the old man giving Eszter an encouraging goodbye nod as he let her and her baby off. As soon as they were on shore, the massive destruction which had taken place only a few weeks before really hit Eszter, now that she was standing in the middle of it all. The parliament building itself was severely damaged, as was the castle on the Buda hill opposite. Much of the rest of city had been completely destroyed. The near total destruction was a tremendous shock for her to see. They were arriving back in their home city, whatever might lay in store for them, but the ruins that were in front of her were of a place unrecognisable from the one she had left.

Eszter cuddled Eva close to her, clutching her bundle of belongings, and started to walk the short distance towards her family's apartment. It was only a few hundred metres to the street behind the parliament where the house with the apartment was, but she had to clamber over rubble, shattered glass and iron girders to make her way there. She had no idea what she would see when she got there, and she proceeded tentatively because of the fear she had that there may be no house remaining. Groups of Soviet troops stood eyeing her as she passed, but she kept her head down and none of them stopped her. She could hear sporadic rifle fire which seemed to be coming mostly from the rooftops towards targets on the ground.

As she turned the corner and entered their street, her heart leaped inside her. Looking down the street, she could see that the building where she had lived with her parents was still standing, in spite of the wide-spread destruction of many other buildings around it. The opposite side of the street had been almost completely destroyed by the war that had raged. Eszter reached the outside of the house and paused for a minute to take in the extensive damage: most of the outside windows were shattered and the front scarred by both small gun fire and large ordnance. But the building itself was at least still standing and appeared to her to be stable. She pushed at the heavy wood door and it opened in front of her. She walked across the courtyard towards her parents' apartment and was overjoyed to see that from the outside at least it seemed to be largely undamaged.

As Eszter stood looking at the outside of the apartment, she heard a noise of a door slamming and saw Hanna the concierge appear up the steps of her basement flat and run towards her. She had seen Eszter arriving through her ground level window. She threw her arms around Eszter and her baby and burst into tears. 'Eszter, you're safe! How pleased I am to see you! Come down to my flat and I will get you the key to your apartment.' Eszter was pleased to see that Hanna – whom she remembered as a friend of her mother's – was still alive and well. In spite of the sadness she felt coming back to her family home empty of her mother and father and the rest of her family, Hanna at least represented one small part of her happier past.

The two women sat in Hanna's apartment and talked together. Eszter could not believe the story that Hanna told her. The city of Budapest had been besieged by Soviet forces for nearly two months since Christmas. The city had been encircled on 26 December by Red Army and Romanian forces. During the siege that followed tens of thousands of civilians had died through starvation and military action.

'It was a terrible time,' Hanna told her. 'All of the families from the flats here fled to the cellars, which were filled with sewage, to hide from the bombs that were raining down around us. We were starving and trapped. We couldn't get out. There were snipers shooting from the top of the buildings on every street corner. From time to time one of the younger men named Franz went out in search of some flour or fresh water for us. On one occasion he came back with some meat he had butchered from one of the many dead horses that were lying in the street. He brought us back the news of the fierce fighting in the streets. A soldier told him that the German army had been ordered by Hitler to 'fight to the death', and they had no choice anyway since there was no chance of escape. There was fighting street by street and even in the sewers which were being used for troop movements to avoid attack from above.

'In the middle of January the German army was withdrawn from our Pest side of the river to entrench in the castle area on Buda Hill, blowing up all the bridges as they did so. The fighting continued until 13 February, when we got news that the Germans had unconditionally surrendered. The Soviet army streamed into the city and there was looting of what was left of it and mass rape by Soviet troops and Hungarian criminals who had been released to the anarchy that reigned. We heard stories of many women and girls being raped, some of them nearby along this very street. Sadly, our brave colleague Franz was shot in the back by a sniper at the entrance to the house as he returned from another expedition to look for food for us. After that we had almost nothing to eat or drink for days and no further news of the conflict.'

'Oh, Hanna – how awful! I had no idea that I would be returning to something like this. I am so pleased you at least are alive and safe. I will do everything I can to help you. Hanna handed Eszter the key to her family apartment and went with her to let her in. There was minor damage on the outside, but miraculously things were largely intact on the inside. A considerable amount of dust and plaster had fallen from the ceiling during the bombing raids, but it did not appear that the flat had been broken into or used during all the terrible conflict. Eszter said a prayer of thanks for that as she started to clean the place up.

CHAPTER 16

February, 1945

Dusk was falling as he walked up the path towards the old farmhouse not far from Brzezinka. Peter stopped at the door to look around. He could see that the place was inhabited; the small garden had been kept up and planted with vegetables and there was smoke coming out of the farmhouse chimney. He could vaguely remember the farmer and his wife who had lived there before the war, although he couldn't recall their names. When he had been posted to work as an SS guard at the Birkenau concentration camp, he realised at once that the camp was on the same land his village of Brzezinka had been. It was not long before he found out that the village had been destroyed and its inhabitants displaced to build the new camp. He was hopeful now that the farmer and his wife who lived close to the village might be able to provide him with some information as to what had happened to the displaced inhabitants, that they might even be able to give him news of his own parents. He prayed that he might find out that they had survived the ransacking of the village, and where they had gone to. He turned back to the door and knocked in hope.

The door was opened by his mother, who stood looking straight at him for a few unbelieving seconds. 'My son, my son!' Irena cried out, falling into his arms in floods of tears, as she dragged him through the door into the living room. His father jumped up from where he was sitting in front of the wood fire and joined in the happy mutual embrace. The three of them stood there locked together in joyful reunion.

Irena broke free at last and, holding her son by the shoulders, looked at him with a mother's questioning, tearful eye. 'We can't believe you are still alive!' she cried. 'Are you well?'

'As well as can be expected, under the circumstances,' Peter replied, teasing his mother in the same way that, as the youngest son, he had always enjoyed doing in the past. For her part, Irena sat her beloved son down in front of the fire and started to mother him – something she had lost all hope of ever having the chance to do again.

'Let me get you something to eat and drink. When did you last have food?' She brought out a bottle of beer and started laying out a meal, such as it was, with the remains of bread, cheese and pickle that she had been keeping for her and Artur's supper that evening.

His father sat opposite him, saying nothing, but looking at him with shining rheumy eyes. Eventually he too found his voice.

'You are very thin, my son. Have you been ill?' his father asked.

'Only from starvation, father,' Peter replied, smiling at his father. The fact was that, even though he had been a member of the SS camp guard, he had not been an officer or a member of the guard's elite, and his rations had been meagre to say the least. He had lost a considerable amount of weight during his time at the camp, not to mention the last months he had spent in solitary confinement. But he did not discuss these details with his father.

As they sat together, Peter told his parents the story of what had happened to him since he had left home with his two brothers, as part of the Polish army to defend the Polish border. Their battalion had been overwhelmed by the German army, after which he was arrested with the other soldiers who had survived the fighting. He was sure that they were all going to be shot. But by luck, he and his brothers got into conversation in German with one of the soldiers guarding them and explained that they were, in fact, German citizens. He and his brothers were separated from the rest of their comrades and brought in front of the officer commanding the troop which had captured them. They were able to show their identity cards, confirming their German citizenship by virtue of their father's birth. After a detailed grilling – in German – the sergeant was satisfied that the story that they were the sons of a German father, working in Poland before the Germans invaded, was accurate. Peter had actually been told by the officer that he could see from his blond hair and blue eyes that he was telling the truth. He was released from detention but immediately enlisted – with no option for dissent – into the Wehrmacht. He found himself fighting on the other side with no possibility to object. After his reprieve, he had served as a private soldier in the Wehrmacht for over four years, before being transferred to the SS as a member of a platoon in one of the Auschwitz camp guard units.

'By the time I was posted to Birkenau, the camp had been completed and I learnt that the inhabitants of Brzezinka had all been displaced from the area. It never occurred to me that you might still be living so close by, so near to where Brzezinka had been. I feared you might be dead, that you might have been killed by the Germans as the village was ransacked.'

Artur and Irena sat listening silently to their youngest son's story, amazed to learn that he had been posted to within a stone's throw of where they now sat, a soldier in the camp nearby over the past few months.

'How was it you were allowed to come looking for us now?' his father asked, astonished by this story.

'I have been very lucky, father. One day while I was on duty at the Birkenau railhead, responsible for guarding the men, women and children as they arrived off the train – Jews, Roma and elderly and disabled people – I was arrested because I allowed a young Hungarian woman with a baby in her arms to escape from the line of prisoners who had fallen out of a wagon. My duty as an SS camp guard was to stand all day at the railhead to the Birkenau camp guarding the poor people who had been arriving in their thousands every day. I was never required to work within the camp itself or, thankfully, to be involved in the 'selection' process of those prisoners who were herded into the death chambers where they were then immediately gassed to death. But I knew what was going on inside from other soldiers in my platoon. I had reached the point where I could not stand it any longer. I could not bear to see this young woman and her baby – who must have been only a few months old – go to their death. She was young and fair, and I thought she would therefore have more chance of surviving.

'I was detained immediately, put in prison and then hauled before my platoon commander at a hastily arranged disciplinary hearing. I felt sure my time had come, that I was about to end up before the firing squad. I was prepared to die. But as it transpired, my commanding officer decided he would be lenient with me and discharged me back to the ranks of the Wehrmacht with a severe reprimand instead. After months in prison, in solitary confinement, I was transported on a truck away from Birkenau. I had no idea whether I was being taken to front-line duties, perhaps even to the Russian front, or even to my death. But during the first night's stop I managed to escape from the barn that I and other prisoners had been locked into, and made my way back here, without being re-captured. I cannot tell you how happy and lucky I am to find you both still alive and living in this old farmhouse so near to where our village of Brzezinka once was.'

After Peter had finished his story, his parents sat there taking it all in. They could not believe what he had been through.

'I don't suppose you have any news for us from your brothers?' his mother asked.

'I'm afraid not, mother,' Peter replied. 'The last time I saw Jan and Marek was after we were captured by the invading Germans and forced to enlist in the Wehrmacht, following our interrogation by the German army officer. I have had no contact with them since then.' He could see that both his parents were disappointed by this news, but were determined not to show this to him in the excitement of their youngest son's safe return to them.

There was a pause in the conversation, as they sat beside each other in front of the fire getting used to the idea that they were back together at last. Something on the floor next to his foot caught Peter's eye; he bent down to pick it up, recognising it at once.

'Where did this come from?' he asked his mother.

'It's a corn doll which was the toy of the baby daughter of a Hungarian girl we were harbouring for some months,' his mother said. 'The little girl must have dropped it on the floor before she and her mother left to return to Budapest last week.' Peter looked at it in amazement. Slowly, without any word of explanation to his mother or father, he placed it deep in the inside pocket of his greatcoat next to the other corn doll he had retrieved from the mud at the railhead in Birkenau, at the moment the girl and her baby had fled for their lives.

CHAPTER 17

I t did not take Peter long to recover his strength. His mother did not stop feeding him and, although they only had the milk and eggs and vegetables which the small farm produced, this was much more than most people in the war-torn country had to sustain them. Many of the population were starving to death as the protracted war went on. He knew that his mother made a point of sharing the food that the she and his father had with him in unequal proportions, seeing that he always got the most. But there was no use protesting to her about this. She would only have gone on favouring him and he knew in his heart that she had a need to show her love for him in this way. He was grateful that he was putting on weight and regaining his strength by the day.

Peter would have liked to have helped his parents by working on the farm. But they all knew that it would be dangerous for him to be seen out on the land. He was therefore essentially confined to the farmhouse and naturally soon started to feel trapped where he was. In spite of himself, he was unable to forget the girl with the small baby, whom he had learnt from his mother was called Eszter. He explained to Irena that she was the very girl that he had met at the railhead at the entrance to Birkenau. The one he had allowed to escape with her baby from the death that awaited them. An act for which he had been put under arrest and imprisoned.

Eszter came in to his dreams every night and thoughts of her occupied much of his waking hours. His sleep was restless with the thought that she was out there somewhere on her own, with her young baby, and probably in grave danger. His desire to search for her and find her grew with each day that passed.

He was standing in the kitchen with his mother, who was preparing soup for their supper one evening. He had peeled the potatoes, which she was now cutting up and stirring in to a broth with some stock she had saved.

'I'm planning to leave for Hungary on Monday, mother,' Peter broke the news to his mother as gently as he could.

'But, my son, you've only been with us for a few weeks, and we cannot bear to lose you again so soon!' his mother cried, breaking down in tears.

Peter held his sobbing mother in his arms. 'I know, mother,' he said, gently stroking her grey hair. 'But I have to go. I have to find the girl I met so briefly, but not so briefly that I fell in love with her. My wish to protect her at that meeting was so strong that by allowing her to escape I nearly lost my life in the process. I need to find out whether perhaps she feels the same about me. I am determined to travel to Budapest to search for her.'

The two of them stood looking at each other.

Finally, his mother sighed: 'I understand, Peter. You are a man and must go where your heart takes you. But do you understand how difficult the road will be between here and Hungary?' – she hesitated, now talking to herself rather than to him – 'I can't believe I am having the same conversation with my youngest son, only a few weeks after having had the same parting plea with the girl he has fallen in love with!' She paused, then spoke to him directly again: 'But in addition to this, have you thought what the consequences for you will be if you are arrested by the Nazis and found to be an escaped German army prisoner? And there is something else I must tell you – something I have not discussed with you yet – the girl Eszter was married to a Hungarian man named Robert just before she and her family were arrested and transported to Birkenau. He is the father of her baby Eva.'

'Don't think I haven't thought about all this mother,' Peter said. 'As far as the journey is concerned, I am determined to take my chance, as she did. As for the other man, perhaps he will not have returned.'

* * *

Soviet armies undertook a massive attack against German occupied Hungary leading to the fall of Budapest in February 1945, after a siege of nearly two months. Peter Leahy hitched a lift on a supply wagon which stopped on the road a few days after the Soviet army had finally taken the city and it took him right in to now Soviet occupied Budapest.

CHAPTER 18

February, 1945

The guards finally ordered them to stop work. The men were so hungry and exhausted that they had in any case long since stopped working properly, although they were not able to make their guards aware of the fact. Any overt display that they were flagging would always be met with a beating; just one blow from a rifle butt might well lead to their death in the emaciated physical state they were in. They had become proficient at pretending to work, without giving any hint to their guards that they were doing so.

Robert laid his spade down by the roadside. He had been labouring in this mine quarry near the town of Vac, some seventy kilometres north of Budapest, ever since he had been rounded up in Budapest for 'labour service'. Since that day he and the other prisoners, something like two hundred men in all, had been treated like slaves by their guards. Their unit of Jewish men had been exposed to extreme cruelty, abuse and brutality. He had witnessed the men who worked in the quarry being beaten daily and sometimes pushed to their deaths off the man-made cliffs and embankments by the gendarmes guarding their 'slaves', as a punishment for the simple fact that they had been perceived not to be working hard enough. If the treatment they were having to endure was not bad enough, these guards were mostly Hungarians themselves, members of the fascist, anti-Semitic Arrow Cross Party.

He had lost count of how many months they had been there and could not imagine how long this was likely to continue. He was resigned to the likelihood that the only way freedom would arrive from this unbearable existence was death from starvation or by violence. He had not forgotten Eszter, the girl he had married only just before his arrest. But they had been together for such a brief time, all that seemed like another life.

The guards were blowing their whistles shrilly and starting to get rough with any prisoner who might not be falling into line promptly enough. The guards were tired themselves and wanted to finish the shift, Robert thought to himself, but they could be nowhere near the total exhaustion and hunger of their prisoners. He fell into line quickly, knowing how dangerous the situation could be at this time of the evening. When their guards were also tired and hungry they often became even more impatient and even more violent towards their prisoners. All the prisoners lined up quickly in their usual four groups of about fifty men in each group, and started to trudge wearily slowly up the hill and back towards the camp. They all hated their captors equally, but were not going to let them know this.

The first group of men arrived at the old barn a few hundred metres from the camp and as they did so they closed ranks to march together in an imperceptibly tighter formation. As the road passed around the corner of the barn, they wheeled to the left in such a way as to merge with the young guard who was positioned there on the corner. The man in front of Robert feigned to stumble to the ground, and as the guard bent forward to drag the man to his feet another prisoner thrust the knife which he had been concealing in his shirt up to its hilt into the guard's chest, entering the space below the man's fifth rib, straight into his heart. The speed of the action was such that the blade was not exposed for long enough for its passage to be reflected by the evening sunlight. The amazed expression on the guard's face they saw was his last before he died instantly and with no sound. As the prisoner caught his falling body under the left armpit, another prisoner thrust his arm under the guard's right armpit, and the comical trio pirouetted to the left and into the open barn door. Robert and the rest of his group continued their march up the hill without breaking step.

The whole event occurred in just a few seconds. The guard's body fell forward with a thump, as it was thrown face down onto the floor in a corner of the barn. In the next second one arc of the pitchfork grabbed by the first prisoner deposited a whole bale of hay, which had been positioned on the shelf above for this purpose, over the body. A further second was enough for both men to make sure that the body was fully covered, and that no further work was necessary to completely disguise its position.

The third group of men had already passed the corner of the barn and was trudging on up the hill. As the final group of fifty men closed ranks and left wheeled, passing as close to the corner of the barn as possible, the two men quietly rolled back out of the barn door into the group as it too trudged back up the hill to the camp. Another of the men towards the back of this group stuck out his foot to push the barn door shut. One of the last men in the group passing the place noted a small pool of bright red blood on the ground, where it had spurted from the guard's mouth as he met his death, and reached out his boot to cover it with some hay and dust from the side of the track. The guards who had been marching the lines of men wearily up the hill back to the camp continued to trudge forwards without looking around as they headed for home, too tired to notice that anything out of the ordinary had been taking place.

As the working gang reached the top of the hill, the gates of the camp were thrown open and the men marched through. They were lined up to attention on the mud parade ground and then counted one by one into the three dormitory blocks by the dormitory guards. As they entered their block, each man in Robert's group collapsed on his back onto his bunk, as they had done every night since they could remember. Not a word passed their lips, but their eyes glinted in defiance at each other as they looked from bunk to bunk in the failing light.

CHAPTER 19

The next morning Robert awoke with a start at about 5 a.m. It was getting light already. The sound of heavy gunfire could be heard very near to their camp and mortar fire was landing from time to time on the camp grounds itself. He jumped out of his bunk and rushed to the door, followed by the rest of the men in his dormitory block. Trying the handle, he found the door unlocked. Looking out, he could see men from other blocks being rounded up by the guards. They were being marched away in single file out of the camp gate. Robert was immediately suspicious about what he saw happening. Why should the guards be moving men out prior to a Soviet attack which might well lead to their liberation?

'Psst!' he said, to his friends Edvard and Jerzy. 'Let's make ourselves scarce!' The three of them jumped off the platform and shuffled on their stomachs to hide in the narrow gap under the dormitory block, from where they lay watching events without being noticed. After only a short pause, they heard volleys of gunshots not too far away. The three men looked at each other. They all knew that this was what Robert had guessed. The Arrow Cross guards were starting to kill the prisoners before the camp was liberated by the Soviet invaders to prevent the prisoners giving evidence of the forced labour, brutality and killings which they had been subjected to all these months.

After only a short time later, Robert could see from where he was lying under the dormitory that the situation had changed. He could hear from the incoming fire that the Soviets were getting very near. The guards had stopped lining up prisoners to be marched outside and shot, but had abandoned this idea and were now running for their own lives, backwards and forwards in disarray. The air was filled with smoke and dust and there was the smell of cordite in the air. The guards were hurriedly throwing equipment on to trucks and jumping into the cabs or climbing onto the back of the trucks. They were now paying no attention whatsoever to the remaining prisoners, who stood around the parade ground watching their preparations for retreat with incredulity. The guards sat looking out of the trucks anxiously, waiting for the last of their colleagues to jump in, their weapons fully loaded and pointing in all directions, ready for the trucks to make their escape from the camp which was now under heavy direct attack. The camp gates were thrown open and the trucks' engines roared into life and accelerated towards the exit. Robert and his two friends crawled back out from under the dormitory block.

In the confusion that was taking place, Robert looked around and saw that the door to the guards' office had been left wide open as they fled. Without drawing attention to himself, he stepped quietly inside. He grabbed open the drawers in the commandant's desk one by one, not really sure what he was looking for. To his amazement, there in the bottom of a drawer he found a large wad of bank notes still with a paper wrap around them. He thrust the money into his shirt and sauntered out into the chaos again. Nobody seemed to have noticed him. The other prisoners were all busy gawking at their captors' retreat and the prison guards themselves were too busy making their escape.

As the last of three trucks of fleeing Arrow Cross guards sped out of the gates a mortar landed right onto the jeep which was bringing up the rear, which exploded into flames. Men were thrown out of the vehicle by the explosion, their bodies lying bleeding and dead all around the jeep. One of the camp gates swung idly on one hinge; the other gate had been completely blown away, the splinters of wood scattered like matchsticks all around the camp entrance. Peter could see the inert corpses lying on the ground where they had been thrown by the blast. There was no sign of any of the camp guards remaining in the compound and the three leading trucks did not come back for their dead comrades.

The prisoners stood on the parade ground watching the scene in disbelief as the drama unfolded before them. After a brief silent pause, the smoke from the incendiaries started to settle and a platoon of Soviet soldiers entered the camp, led by their officer, fanning out around the parade ground. The prisoners raised their arms in surrender above their heads and turned to face the wall of their wooden dormitory blocks. One by one Soviet soldiers passed along the lines of surrendering prisoners, checking that none of them had any weapons on them. The search did not take long; the pitifully thin men were scarcely clothed in rags and had nowhere to conceal any weapons, even if they had any, which they clearly did not. Robert held his breath as one of the soldiers searched him for weapons. The man was talking to one of the other soldiers as he did so and barely touched Robert, only intent on making sure that there was nothing metallic inside his clothing, quickly passing on to the next prisoner. The cursory search was completed within only a few minutes and the prisoners were stood down at ease and directed to return to their dormitories. After they had re-entered their dormitory, Robert patted his bundle of bank notes inside his shirt and noticed with relief that none of the doors were being locked again behind them.

Small arms fire continued to be heard outside for the next half hour or so, presumably, Robert thought to himself, the invading Soviet armies mopping up the remaining fleeing camp guards. It was not until the next day that he and the rest of the imprisoned forced labourers learnt that the liberation of the prison camp was just one exercise in a massive attack against German occupied Hungary by Soviet armies which was to lead to the fall of Budapest in a week or so later in February 1945.

For a few days Robert and the other the men stayed in their dormitories, afraid to show their faces without being invited outside, and waited to see what the Soviet invaders proposed to do with them. The Soviet soldiers continued to feed the prisoners at least, which seemed to be a good sign. After a few days, however, the men were lined up on the parade ground and told that they were all free to leave. The Soviet officer in charge told them that they did not have enough food to continue to feed them, and that when they left the camp they would have to fend for themselves.

As soon as he heard this news, Robert did not hesitate. He'd had enough of 'this bloody war'. He wanted to forget the whole of the time he had spent wasting his life in captivity; the forced labour, starvation and physical beatings. He was going straight to a bar when he reached Budapest. Not only did he need a drink, he told himself, he intended to celebrate his freedom at last and have as many drinks as he liked.

Robert was the first to stride out through the camp gates and head south down the road away from Vac and towards Budapest, about seventy kilometres away. He didn't look back. He patted the large wad of money which was now safely stored inside his trouser belt. He had every intention of drinking it wisely.

CHAPTER 20

It did not take Robert many days to walk back down the road along the east bank of the River Danube from the town of Vac to the outskirts of Budapest. When he reached the suburbs at Űjpest he stopped at a bar to rest and considered where he should go next. He ended up staying there for most of the day, drinking until he was very drunk. The months he'd spent subject to forced labour and constant beatings in the internment camp at Vac had damaged him severely. It had affected his mind as well as his body. He was aware that he did not feel right in his mind any more. The only way that he found he was able to control the terrors tearing his brain apart was to get drunk and remain drunk, which he was almost continuously now. In his more lucid moments he was able to realise that this was not a cure for his mental torment. It only suppressed the terrors and postponed the time when he would have to banish them from his thoughts if he was going to survive and re-build his life.

At the end of his day's heavy drinking he rented a room above the bar. He staggered drunk up the stairs about midnight, fell onto the bed and slept well into the afternoon of the next day. He was unbearably thirsty when he awoke and bent down at the tap slaking his thirst over many minutes. He paid the landlord what he owed from the large wad of bank notes he had taken from the camp office and walked out into the sunshine towards the centre of Budapest.

It was late evening when he arrived in the city. He went into another bar in a basement in a poor part of town. Being underground, the place had largely avoided the destruction which had taken place in the city above it. He ordered some food and started drinking again. Much later, he slept in a room above that bar, as drunk as he had been the night before. The next day he climbed into the ruins of a building which had been badly damaged in the fighting which had taken place and found a room where he could sleep. There was no roof above him and he lay looking up at the night sky as he tried to sleep. The weather was dry, at least, but it was bitterly cold and he had no blanket or thick coat to cover him. The rest of the building was deserted, probably because its previous occupants had either been killed or had fled the place because it was in danger of collapsing completely. He didn't care. He felt that he would not mind if the whole lot collapsed on him and killed him as he slept there. That would at least be one way out of his miserable existence.

The next day and the day after that, Robert visited one or other of the bars still operating in the area where he found himself. He would stay at the bar until it closed at night and then drag himself drunk back to his room in the bombed out building. He vaguely started to wonder what had happened to the girl Eszter he had met and married not long before he was taken away to the forced labour camp. He was aware that during the time he had spent in the labour camp he had hardly given her much thought. He shrugged to himself as he realised this. After all, for most of his waking days – and for many of his sleeping hours – the only thing on his mind had been the fear of death and the remote hope of keeping alive. He guessed there was a high chance that she had not survived the war. But the way he felt now, numbed by his life and any thoughts he might have for the future, he did not care too much if he never saw her again.

CHAPTER 21

March, 1945

Eszter bent over concentrating on the flagstones as she swept the courtyard outside their apartment block with an old besom broom. She had been working hard since she arrived back in her apartment, slowly cleaning the place and getting it back into a habitable state for herself and her young child. As she stood up to take a break, leaning on the broom and rubbing the base of her aching back with her right hand, she noticed a man standing staring at her from across the yard. She looked straight at the young man. He seemed familiar. Where had she met him before?

Peter walked slowly up to her and held out one of his clenched fists in front of her. With a broad smile on his face, he slowly unfurled his fingers to reveal the small corn doll nestling in the palm of his hand.

Eszter looked at the man, amazed. 'Where did you get that?' She demanded.

'You know where I got it,' Peter replied. 'I picked it up from the mud at the Birkenau railhead where you dropped it as you ran off!'

'Look,' he said, opening the palm of his other hand to reveal an identical corn doll. 'I've even got her sister. This is the one I found on the floor of my parents' living room, shortly after you left them to come back to Hungary. I was so pleased to hear from my mother and father that you had survived the escape and had been hiding safe with them. It's an incredible coincidence that by chance you took refuge in my parents' house, without knowing I was one of their missing sons. My name's Peter, by the way.'

Eszter took a deep breath in and cried: 'You are Irena and Artur's son Peter? Is this true? I cannot believe this! And you have come all this way to find me. You haven't been out of my thoughts since that day!' She ran to greet him.

'It's true: I am Peter!' he smiled, holding out his arms to wrap them round her and hold her tightly.

Eszter and Peter sat together in the apartment late on into the evening, holding hands and getting to know each other.

'How on earth did you find me here in this destroyed city of Budapest?' Eszter asked him.

'My mother remembered you talking to her about your family apartment in Budapest and describing the street it was in. You had told Irena that the apartment was on the ground floor of a house in a street immediately behind the parliament building and not far from the basilica. Although I didn't have your exact address, as soon as I entered the city I searched for a street in an area that fitted the description you had given my mother. It wasn't easy to work out where this might be on account the destruction of the city from the bombing. Incredibly, however, the parliament building and the basilica were still standing, although badly damaged. Whenever I found people who were in buildings behind the basilica which were more or less standing, I asked them whether they had seen a young woman with a baby who had only recently arrived in the area. It didn't take me long to find a building in this street which at least was still standing and a helpful old lady who could direct me to you. And here I am!'

Eszter only broke away from Peter long enough to bring him a glass of wine and some bread and cheese for them both. As he ate, she sat on the sofa contentedly breast feeding baby Eva next to him. The hours that seemed to fly by were of no consequence. They were both hungry to get to know each other and learn each other's stories. They listened to one another with the wide-eyed amazement of newly found lovers. The joy for them both was not diminished by the fact that Eszter talked freely to Peter about her marriage to Robert and her short time with him. Although she did not say so openly, there was an assumption that he must surely be dead, and Peter was aware that she talked about him in the past.

CHAPTER 22

March, 1945

E szter busied herself laying the table for breakfast. She had been up for some hours, had already fed Eva and cleaned the kitchen. Peter was still asleep, breathing deeply as he had done every night since he'd arrived nearly two weeks before. She knew he had been exhausted by his ordeal of imprisonment and his journey to Budapest by foot through war-torn country, and she continued to let him sleep until he was ready to wake each day, which was often not until late in the morning.

After only a day or two Peter took it upon himself to start helping her with the apartment. Although Eszter's family apartment had not been broken into and ransacked or taken over during the time it lay empty, Peter nevertheless found things that needed repairing and mending, and would venture out into the local district searching for items he required for this purpose. There were many houses around them that had been seriously damaged and even totally destroyed. Peter would come back with pieces of wood he had rescued from bombed out properties nearby and set to work with hammer and nails making the ceiling safe and mending bits of furniture. He also took to exploring the local area to get to know his new surroundings, in spite of the near total destruction of the city. He foraged for supplies and brought back what bread and other bits of food he could find, which usually was not much.

Whenever Peter left her and Eva alone for an hour or two, Eszter could not help but worry about his safety. She knew he could look after himself when on his own, but worried that he might be caught up in fighting that was still taking place; there were pockets of resistance, with gunfire breaking out across the city from time to time as the local Hungarian militia continued to conduct a rear-guard action against the occupying Russian invasion. He could be unlucky enough to be hit by a stray bullet, although she knew the chances of this were remote.

Within a few weeks of finding each other, Eszter and Peter settled into their lives together. Eszter could not believe that she had found a new man who was so much in love with her. She remembered the day when she and Irena were doing the washing up together and Irena started to tell her about her missing sons. Irena had described Peter, the youngest of her three boys, as a romantic, more interested in reading poetry and making up stories. He certainly revealed himself to Eszter to be all of those things. She had never met a more romantic man before. He delighted in the fact that many of her parents' large collection of books were still intact in the bookshelves around the living room. Although many of them were written in Hungarian, of course, there were quite a lot of German books as well. He took these over for his own enjoyment and read them avidly, very often reading out loud to her as well late at night. He would make up stories and bits of his own poems which he would read aloud to both herself and baby Eva. Eva would sit entranced, listening intently to the stories he was weaving. In spite of the on-going war that continued to rage in Europe and the Soviet occupation of Budapest, they were both very happy to be together.

That night they lay together on the bed naked, in each other's arms. He took her hand and guided it down to him. He was erect and hard. Very gently, he parted her legs with his two hands and lifted her up. He entered her slowly but deeply, taking his time. Giving her time. All the while talking softly to her. Making sure she wanted him as much as he wanted her. She had never experienced anything like this with the only other man she had been with, her husband Robert. And that was for such a short time.

He was deep inside her and she opened up towards him, wanting him so much. As he came to his climax, she came too. She cried with joy, tears running down her face.

Later, as they lay there together, he continued to stroke her lovingly.

'You don't feel guilty about this?' he asked her.

'About Robert? No. I'm sure he must be dead,' she admitted for the first time. 'Even if he survived the labour camp and escaped back here, it is very unlikely he would have survived the siege of the city. He would have come straight back here if he had.' She turned to him and kissed him on the lips. He held her closely as they slept in each other's arms.

From then on, neither of them had any hesitation that they wanted to live together. They didn't discuss the fact. They didn't have to. Eszter welcomed

Peter as her new husband and he took up the role easily, taking great care of Eszter and little Eva, who was starting to take her first faltering steps, to the joy and amusement of them both. They knew that their time together could turn out to be as brief as that which Eszter had had with Robert – that Peter too could be arrested and taken away at any time if his presence in Budapest was discovered.

CHAPTER 23

April, 1945

One early spring morning, Eszter was in the front room, clearing the table from the night before and picking up from the floor the wooden toys Peter had made Eva. Peter had gone out, on his daily search for food for them. Little Eva was singing happily in the courtyard, where she was playing with her corn dolls. Through the open front door, Eszter could hear her child singing bits of Peter's songs she had picked up from him and talking baby talk to the dolls and sharing her thoughts with them. There was a pause in the little girl's pretend conversation. Eszter looked up as Eva came running unsteadily into the house gripping her dolls close to her chest.

'Mummy, Mummy, who's that man?' Eva cried, hiding behind her mother and holding on to her skirt tightly.

Eszter looked up to see Robert standing framed in the door in front of her. As she stood transfixed, Robert slowly stretched his arms out towards her, a broad grin on his face. He was swaying slightly and almost leering at her. Eszter turned to Eva. 'Hush, child' she said. 'Don't be afraid. He's your father.'

Eszter walked towards her husband and gave him a hug, looking to one side as she did so. 'Can I come in?' Robert asked her, kissing her tentatively on the forehead, perhaps sensing Eszter's unexpected unease at his return.

'Of course,' Eszter replied, leading him through into the kitchen and inviting him to sit down at the table. 'Would you like something to eat and drink?'

'Yes, please. I've had very little to eat since escaping from the internment camp at Vac two months ago. It's taken me all this time to find my way back to Budapest and locate you in your parents' old apartment. I could finish off a bottle of wine, if you have one,' he added as an afterthought.

Eszter busied herself at the stove, heating up the remains of their soup from the night before, her brain whirring inside her head as she did so. How was she going to tell Robert about Peter living here, before Peter returned home? She reached up and took the only bottle of red wine they had from the shelf above the stove. She automatically ladled some soup into a dish and, as she turned to hand it to Robert, Peter walked in through the front door. Robert looked up at him with surprise, and then, more slowly, turned to look back at Eszter.

'Who is this man?' was all he said.

Eszter put the bowl of soup and wine bottle on the table. She sat down next to Robert and took his hand, while Peter still stood motionless, transfixed in the door frame. As he stood there, little Eva walked quietly to Peter's side and stood next to him, reaching up to hold his hand.

'A lot has happened since you were rounded up and taken off for labour service, Robert. I realised I was pregnant very shortly after you had left. This is our little girl Eva' – she pointed at the child – 'who was born in the apartment here. I had a very difficult labour, but my mother and aunt saw me through it together. I was so happy to be given the gift of a lovely daughter, but just wished that I could get news to you to tell you about her. And now here you are, and can see her for yourself. Eszter turned in her chair to smile at Eva, who was still standing holding Peter's little finger with her tiny hand.'

Robert sat silently, making no comment on the story that Eszter was telling him. He poured himself a large glass of red wine and drank it down in one go. Without hesitation, he filled his glass again.

'Soon after Eva's birth,' Eszter continued, trying her hardest to engage him, 'I and my family were arrested by the Gestapo because we were Jews and transported from here to the concentration camp at Birkenau in Poland. It was a terrible experience, threatened by violence at any minute and surrounded by dead and dying people. I am certain my mother and father, sister and aunt were murdered in the camp. By an extraordinary chance, I had a very lucky escape with Eva at the camp entrance and ran for freedom. Eventually, we managed to find refuge with an elderly couple who lived on a farm not far from Birkenau. Peter here is one of their sons. I hid with his parents for nearly ten months before making my way alone with Eva safely back to Budapest.

'After you were taken away for labour service I received no news of you whatever. After about six months with the two kind old people, I knew I had to return to Hungary and still hoped then that I might find you alive and well.

When I eventually arrived way back here in Budapest, I found that you were still missing and that no one knew anything about your whereabouts. I feared you must be dead. I assumed that you too had not survived the fighting, either during the German invasion of Hungary or the Soviet invasion that followed.'

Eszter paused, realising as she did so that, in telling Robert the story of what had happened to them since he had disappeared from their lives, she had omitted to mention that Peter was also the SS guard who had given herself and Eva the chance to escape from the railhead at Birkenau, had allowed them to live. She wasn't going to complicate matters further by adding that detail now. She could sense that her account of what had happened to her was not convincing her husband.

Robert continued to sit staring at her, taking in the implications of everything he had heard, but saying nothing. He pulled the cork from the bottle and poured himself another large glass of wine. In two swigs, he had finished the glass and poured another, empting the bottle.

CHAPTER 24

Later, after Robert had left, but not before making clear his intention to return, Eszter and Peter were alone together once more.

'Oh, Peter! Tell me. How can I make this choice?'

'It's been made for us, my Love. He's the man you married and the father of your child . . .'

Peter climbed the stairs slowly and started to collect his small amount of possessions together, wrapping them into a bundle with one of Eszter's shawls. He had feared this possibility, had already considered the consequences, and knew he had to leave Eszter to choose between himself and her husband. He walked back down stairs with a heavy heart.

'I will love you always,' he said, holding Eszter tightly in his arms. 'Keep safe.' He kissed her one last time, turned and walked out of the door. Eszter stood looking after him, tears running down her cheeks, unable to speak.

* * *

Over the next few weeks Eszter tried her hardest to be faithful to her husband and the marriage vows she had made to him. But however hard she tried, she was unable to banish Peter from her heart. Robert did not make it easy for her. He remained angry with her for the fact that she had presumed him dead so readily, and taken another man so easily. Almost as a threat to his wife, it seemed to her, he continued to drink heavily. He did not mention Peter once and never asked how it was that Eszter had met up with him.

'Please, Robert – don't be angry with me anymore. Peter has gone away and there is no reason for you to continue to feel jealous,' Eszter said at last to her husband one evening as they finished supper.

'Wouldn't any man be angry to come back from war and find another man in bed with his wife?' Peter shouted at her, banging his knife and fork on the table. 'It's not as easy to accept as you seem to want it to be. I'm going out.'

Peter left the apartment, slamming the front door behind him. The noise woke Eva, who started crying for her mother from the bedroom. Eszter went to comfort her. She sat on the child's cot with tears of sadness and humiliation running down her face.

That night Robert did not return home until well after midnight. He had been drinking heavily and his breath smelt of liquor. He jumped into bed next to Eszter still partly clothed and forced himself on her. When he had finished, he rolled off her and fell deeply asleep. For her part, Eszter lay there for most of the rest of the night with a great emptiness inside her which bore down as heavily as the dark night around her.

* * *

From then on things only got worse. They had no money and she had to beg for help from their neighbours. Hanna at least was someone that Eszter could escape to and she would spend time with her now and again, sitting in her apartment in the basement.

'I'm sorry I have no food or drink to share with you and your baby,' Hanna told Eszter the first time Eszter went to visit her after Robert arrived back. 'You know I would if I could, but I am starving myself.' Eszter nodded, understanding.

'What is the news of your father and mother and sister?' Hanna asked, as tactfully as she could. She hadn't liked to ask Eszter personal questions about her family when she had first returned back to the apartment, assuming that the news would not be good. She did not want Eszter to have to tell her what she and her baby had experienced after they were taken away that night, until Eszter was ready to share the story with her herself. She had sensed as soon as she arrived back that Eszter was traumatised by what she had endured. But now at least it seemed one way of diverting the discussion away from the hunger they were both experiencing.

Once Hanna had broken the ice, Eszter told her everything that had happened to them. Hanna was shocked and very saddened to hear Eszter's story about how her father, mother, sister and aunt had been murdered in the concentration camp at Birkenau.

'I knew that it was your neighbours Gabor and Klara Szabo who reported you all to the Gestapo as being Jews. I was at home when they broke in through the front door that night. I looked out of my basement window and saw Szabo in the courtyard pointing out your apartment to the armed soldiers. There was nothing an old lady like me could do to stop them. I saw them leading you all away roughly out into the street. I cannot believe that the whole of your family was arrested with no trial and were taken to be murdered because of your religion.' She sat still, holding Eszter's hand.

'It will be no consolation to you if I tell you that the Szabos were arrested themselves for black-marketing about three months after you were taken away,' Hanna continued, after a while. 'Nothing has been heard from them since. I hope they rot in hell!'

'You do know that I would never do anything to betray the fact that you have returned to the authorities?' Hanna said, after a pause. Eszter nodded at her. 'And I am sure there is no one left in the building now that is likely to betray you either,' Hanna did her best to reassure her.

They sat together, hand in hand. Hanna was aware that, now that the Russians were in control of the city, it was unlikely in any case that they would be interested in the fact that Eszter and Eva had arrived back in Budapest having escaped from the Nazi concentration camp at Birkenau.

CHAPTER 25

Eszter was getting desperate. Apart from a few low value filler coins left in the tin on the mantelpiece above the fire, she had no money. Robert did nothing to help earn money for her and Eva, and stayed out most of the day and much of the night. When he did come home late into the night, he was almost always drunk. Eszter had no idea where he had got the money from to buy drink – she had not given him a cent – and did not have the courage to confront him about where he got his money from for fear that he might abuse her physically if she did so. She suspected he might have stolen the money he had from somewhere or someone.

She was so hungry she feared she might not be far from starvation. There were still carcasses of dead horses in the streets, but these had all been butchered for meat, and what was left was now in a putrid condition and not fit to eat. She did her best to keep drinking plenty of water and feeding herself the handfuls of greens she brought back from her trips to the single market that was operating, along with potatoes, when she could get some. The greens were hardly nutritious, mostly the discarded outer leaves of cabbages that had been swept up off the floor, dried up and dirty, which the stallholder often gave her without asking for payment. She was a kind woman who was sensitive to the needs of the young woman and her baby. Eszter would wash them for a long time under the tap and then boil them until they were soft. She was becoming resigned to the possibility that, having escaped from death in the gas chambers of Birkenau, she might be facing her own death by starvation, alone in the apartment. She knew that this was becoming more and more possible. But what she could not bear to consider was that her death would mean the end for little Eva as well. Every morning she would wake with the baby nuzzling her breast, afraid that her milk may have finally dried up.

Eszter started to search the apartment for money that might have been hidden somewhere by her parents before their arrest. But she found none. What she did come across, however, were some pieces of her mother's jewellery. These were hidden in a false compartment at the back of a chest of drawers. Her mother had wrapped the pieces tightly in a piece of cloth and tied this up with string. She lifted the little parcel out carefully and took it to the table where she unwrapped it and examined the contents.

Inside the cloth she found all the pieces of jewellery her mother had ever owned. There were a number of rings – two silver rings, a gold ring and an ornate porcelain ring with a large stone in the middle. She had no idea if this was precious or not. There were three different bracelets – one matching the porcelain ring – and a silver tiara inlaid with stones. She could see a silver mark on the back of that. There were also about six pairs of pretty earrings. She thought that the tiara was something that her mother had had handed down to her by her mother; she remembered seeing an old sepia picture of her grandmother who was wearing the same tiara on her head. She wasn't sure how much these pieces were worth, but she knew she now had no option but to trade them in for herself and her baby, if they were to survive. Eszter bundled the pieces of jewellery back into the cloth, tied it up again and placed the precious parcel in the linen bag she used to bring vegetables from market. Eva was sleeping quietly. She did not want to disturb her if possible, so she picked her up in in her arms very gently and walked out in to the street.

Eva remembered that there was a pawnbroker's shop only a few hundred metres away in Kiraly Street. It was in the basement of a building with steps directly down from the street level, like a lot of other enterprises that existed in the surprising underworld economy which took place beneath the city streets of Budapest. It had been owned by a Jewish man called Binyamin, who was friendly with her father. She had heard her father speak of him as a kind man, one who could be relied on to give a fair price for whatever he bought and not a man to exploit people unfairly.

When she reached the place where the pawnbroker's shop had been, she noticed that the brass sign had been taken down. Instead, there was a piece of board on the door confirming the shop was still operating as a pawnbroker's. She peered in to the top of a window which was visible from street level and saw that there was a candle alight in the room below. Eva pushed at the door which opened easily, ringing a low pitched bell as it did so, and walked slowly down the rickety wooden steps. Inside, the room was as gloomy as a dungeon, lit only dimly by the single candle on the table. Sitting in the circle of candlelight, an unkempt man with a dirty beard was pawing over some pieces of silver with a magnifying glass in his right eye. There was barely enough light for him to work by.

'Can I help you, dear?' he said, with a guttural cough, looking sideways at her.

'Can I speak to Binyamin, if he's around, please,' Eva asked.

'That thieving Jew's not here anymore!' the man croaked, looking at her aggressively, and spat onto the floor. 'Nazi's took him away, and not before time. I hope he's burning in hell with the rest of them. I'm in charge here now. Miki's the name. Take a seat, my dear,' he said pointing to the chair across his table. 'What you got?'

Eszter disliked the man immediately. She could sense that he was crooked and she was repulsed by his hatred for Jews. Even so, she knew she had no choice at the moment but to do business with him. Reluctantly, she reached into her linen bag, brought out the cloth parcel and unwrapped it carefully on the table in front of the man. Without being invited, the man grabbed the pieces, sorting them through roughly and placing them into one of three small piles.

'Give you a three hundred pengő for the tiara,' he said, 'a couple of hundred for the two rings here,' pointing to the second pile. 'Rest's not worth nothin'.'

Eva's eyes filled with tears, tears of both despair and rage.

'That's not fair!' she cried. 'I know my mother's things are worth a lot more than that. I need to be paid the proper rate in order to be able to feed myself and my baby. As she added the last comment, she felt cheap for doing so, but knew she had to try something to get a fairer price for her mother's jewellery. However, the man was completely unmoved by her appeal to him. He did not even cast a glance towards Eva who lay sleeping in her arms.

''S what it is,' the man said shrugging. Slowly he reached down into a drawer in his desk and counted out a handful of coins, pushing them across the desk towards her.

Eva stared with hate at the man. Then, very slowly, she gathered the coins into her purse, leaving the bits of jewellery in the piece of cloth on the table, and stood up and walked back up the stairs to the street with Eva in her arms without saying a further word.

CHAPTER 26

Peter walked up the path to the farmhouse door for the second time in a few months. This time, his footsteps were heavy, as was his heart. He knocked quietly and, after a pause, his mother opened the door.

'Oh, Peter, I'm so pleased to see you! Thank god you are safe. Come on in.' Peter kissed his mother on the cheek, entered the room and sat down in front of the fire. Irena sat beside him.

'Did you find your girl, Eszter? Was she alive and well with her little daughter in Budapest?'

'Yes, mother. Eszter and Eva are well. They survived the journey from here back to Budapest and are living in their old family apartment in the city. Budapest has been almost destroyed during the fighting which took place when the city was under siege by the Russians, but luckily the building in which the apartment is has suffered very little damage. Eszter and I are very much in love, and I was living there together with her and her baby for a few weeks. But her husband Robert came back one day, after Eszter had had no news from him at all since he was taken into forced labour. She had assumed that he had died in the labour camp. As you can understand, I had no choice but to leave Eszter and Eva, which is why I have come back here.' Irena could see how upset he was about leaving Eszter.

'I'm so sorry, son. I am so sorry for you.' Peter nodded to his mother, who sat looking at him with silent glazed eyes.

'Where is father?' he said, looking around the room.

'Artur died two months ago, Peter,' Irena replied in a whisper.

'Oh, mother, I'm so sad!' Peter cried, taking his frail old mother in his arms. 'I wish I'd been here to comfort you.'

'It has been very lonely for me,' Irena said. 'I suppose it was not so unexpected. He had been fading away slowly for a while, even before you came back to us before. At least he died peacefully in his sleep. I found him dead in bed next to me when I woke in the morning. He was laid to rest the same day. Franz, the farmer from down the hill came and dug his grave in a plot behind the farmhouse here. He and his wife Anna have been very kind.'

Peter sat with his mother, comforting her and talking to her quietly about the fond memories he had of his father, a hard-working man with devotion to his wife and family who had lead his life with courage. After a while, he let go of her hand and stood up.

'Do you mind if I go and see him?' he asked Irena.

'Of course not, son,' his mother replied. 'It is a comfort for me to know he is laid to rest in the land behind the house. I visit him a number of times every day and speak to him. I know he is still listening from wherever he is and would like to hear you voice.'

Peter went slowly out of the back door of the farmhouse and walked reverently to the fresh grave with its simple wooden cross marking the spot where his father lay. He stood with his head bowed for some time, not talking to his father as his mother had suggested, but remembering the many happy times they had had together.

Finally he raised his head and said simply: 'I love you, Dad.' He looked across the farm land at the winter sun setting in the west and walked slowly back indoors to be with his mother again.

* * *

Peter stayed with his mother from then on, putting all his energy in to sorting out the farm and looking after his mother as best as he could. He consoled himself that this was the best way of getting over his memories of Eszter and, anyway, was what any decent son should do.

CHAPTER 27

August, 1945

Eszter sat on the step outside the front door of her apartment, gently rocking Eva in her arms. The little girl had been crying to her mother in hunger, and this was the only way that Eszter could show her baby her love. She had no food to give her daughter, and her mother's milk had finally dried up. She looked down in despair at Eva. Her baby was losing weight: her arms and legs were pitifully thin, her skin loose and her ribs protruded from her chest above her concave abdomen. Eszter knew that she herself was also now woefully thin.

Eszter had become tired of begging to the stallholders of every market she visited for scraps of greens and bread for herself and her baby, carrying Eva in her arms as a way of appealing to the man or woman's heart. She hated herself for using Eva as a begging tool in this way, but it was the only tactic left to her. She was too afraid to sit on the pavement of one of the larger streets, openly begging to passers-by. She did not feel any safer now that the city was under Soviet occupation than she had when the Gestapo had been carrying out their reign of terror. She still feared that bringing attention to herself and her baby could just as quickly result in her being exposed to violence from the occupying soldiers. But she knew that she and Eva were now both near to death from starvation.

Eszter looked up to see a small boy running towards her, waving something in his hand in the air. She didn't recognise him as one of the local children. He was puffing heavily and had obviously been running fast.

'I've got a letter for you, Miss,' he said in a high-pitched voice, handing Eva a folded piece of paper. 'Sir would like you to visit him straight away.' With that, he ran back across the courtyard and out of the building.

Eszter was surprised. She couldn't imagine who might be writing to her here in her parents' apartment. As far as she was aware there was nobody else in Budapest, apart from Hanna and her immediate neighbours, who knew of her presence here.

Slowly she unfolded the piece of paper and read the letter written on it:

'Dear Miss Eszter,' it read, 'I would be obliged if you would visit me at my office at 16 Paulay Ede Street. I have some information which will be to your advantage. Yours sincerely, Arno Claussen, Attorney at Law.'

Eszter had no idea what this could mean, what the letter was all about. She wondered if it could be a trap, a trick by the authorities to catch her. But she could not imagine that they would employ silly games like this to catch her out. If they had realised who she was and that she was back in the city at this address, they would surely have just come and arrested her, as they did all of her family including herself a year ago. Whatever the letter was about, she decided that it just might mean what it said, that it might be genuine. She had nothing to lose. She got up carefully so as not to disturb Eva and walked unsteadily down the steps to Hanna's flat in the basement with the baby still in her arms. She was very weak herself and unable to move fast. Hanna opened the door to them.

'Would you mind looking after Eva for me for an hour or so, Hanna? I've got an appointment to go to.'

'Of course dear,' Hanna said, gently taking the sleeping baby from Eszter's arms.

'You go carefully, dear,' Hanna said, eyeing her frail young neighbour with concern. Eszter thanked her and walked away across the courtyard. Hanna had sensed that something was up, although Eva had given her no indication as to where she was going.

Eszter found the address without any problem. Paulay Ede Street was a narrow street running behind the main thoroughfare of Andrassy Avenue, not so far from her apartment. She stood outside the door to number sixteen, which was painted dark green. On the wall was a brass plate which read 'Claussen and Groenwold, Attorneys at Law'. So the writer of the letter she had just received did exist, at least. She rang the bell.

There was a shuffling behind the door, then the sound of bolts being released. A key turned in the lock. The door opened to reveal an old man with whiskers looking over his half-moon glasses.

'Can I help you?' the old man asked.

'I'm Eszter,' she said.

'Ah, Eszter. Yes, do come in.' The man threw the door open to let her in, then bolted it again after she had entered. He sat down at the large director's desk in his office, inviting her to take the seat opposite him.

'I'm Arno Claussen. You don't know me, but I was your father's lawyer for many years.' He hesitated. 'I and my wife Hanneke were so sorry to hear that your father and mother had been arrested and taken away by the Gestapo last year and subsequently transported to the concentration camp at Auschwitz. We were very fond of them both and considered them true friends.'

Eszter was taken aback. 'How do you know about this?' she asked him.

'It's better for me not to divulge the source of my information, my dear. Let's just say that there were still lines of communication that existed in the city in spite of the iron fist of the Gestapo. The same sources, indeed, that still exist now that the Soviets have an equal control over all our lives and brought to my attention the fact that you had recently returned alone with your child to your parents' apartment.' Eva looked at the man amazed that he could have obtained so much information about what had befallen her family.

'Well, since you know all that, I can tell you that I and my baby Eva – who was born only just over two months before in our apartment here in Budapest – were also arrested at the same time as my parents, along with my sister, uncle aunt. We were forced by gunpoint on to the cattle wagon train to Birkenau, to where we were transported with hundreds of other Jews and Roma, disabled, ill and dying people. You cannot imagine how it was. But by an extraordinary chance of luck, I and my baby Eva were allowed by one of the guards to escape at the railhead to Birkenau. I still don't know how we managed to get away without being shot by the machine gun fire that opened up at us from the camp lookout towers as I ran away. My mother and father and other family members were not so lucky. I am certain they were put to death with all the others after being forced into the gas chambers that day.'

Claussen looked at Eva with distress. She could see that there were tears in his eyes.

'I'm so sorry for you Eva,' he said. 'I'm so sorry to learn this news about the deaths of your parents, who were my dear friends. But I had already assumed from what I and my colleagues knew about the terrible murders that were taking place in these camps that this must have been what had happened to them.' He paused for a moment of reflection, and then cleared his mind.

'But now to the reason I invited you here,' Claussen said, composing himself. 'I believe you may have reached your twenty-first birthday by now. Am I correct?'

'Yes, Mr Claussen, I am twenty-three years old already,' Eva replied.

'Good,' Claussen clapped his hands together softly. 'Then I have some news for you.'

'Your father took out a trust in your name when you were a young girl. He wrote it with my assistance; it was signed by your father and witnessed by myself and my assistant and the document has been kept safely in my archives since. It grants money that shall be paid to you on reaching the age of twenty-one, which has clearly well passed. How are you off for money, if I may be direct enough to ask?'

'I have nothing', Eva replied. 'I sold all of my mother's jewellery that I found, but was swindled by a beast of a man in Kiraly Street. What little money I got from him has long been spent. Eva and I are starving.'

'I thought as much,' Claussen said, looking at the desperately thin young woman over his spectacles in a paternal fashion. 'Luckily, at the same time as signing the trust, your father lodged the money for you in cash with me for safe keeping. It has been sitting in my secret safe here since. I fear that had it been deposited in the bank it would likely have been commandeered by the Nazis or stolen without trace somehow in these times of trouble. Even more fortuitously, he converted the money he was bequeathing you into US dollars before he gave it to me, which protected it from the hyperinflation that was to affect the pengő. Your inheritance from this trust can be available to you without delay. It is not a fortune, but has at least not reduced in value as it would have if he had given it to me in Hungarian forints. It will be enough to keep you and your child fed and cared for for a few years at least. Leave me to sort things out and, if you would like to call back tomorrow at the same time, I will have the money for you. In the meantime, won't you join me and my wife Hanneke to lunch?' He stood up and invited her to follow him into their apartment behind his office.

Eszter was amazed and overjoyed by what she was hearing. She said a silent prayer to her father for having come to her rescue, for saving the lives of herself and her baby in this unexpected way.

She walked with Mr Claussen through the door into his apartment, where his wife Hanneke was waiting there to greet her, standing in her apron next to the table which was already laid. The couple had clearly anticipated inviting her for lunch. She kissed Eszter on the cheek as if she were her own daughter and sat her down to eat.

For the first time in months Eszter enjoyed her first real meal. The Claussen's could not have been kinder to her, feeding her well but not wanting to over-feed her in her starving state.

'As you can see, Eszter,' Arno Claussen admitted to her, 'in spite of the rationing and food scarcity generally, we are lucky enough to have access to plenty to eat. More than enough, in fact,' he said, inviting Eva to have a second bowl of beef soup. The taste of a proper meat soup was like heaven to Eva, but she was careful not to eat too much at one go, having heard about the dangers of going from starvation to plenty too quickly.

'You are aware that I and my wife are Jewish, too, Eszter?' Mr Claussen said to her at the end of the meal.

'I had wondered,' Eva replied politely.

'You are probably also wondering how it is that we escaped being arrested for our faith while the Gestapo were here in Budapest?' Claussen said to her.

'The truth is, we don't know ourselves why we were spared, when so many of our Jewish friends and colleagues were arrested and disappeared without trace. It may be that the fact that we are Dutch by extraction helped, and perhaps the fact that we have very many contacts in the city still and not a small number of people who depend on my legal services. But that did not help your poor father and mother did it, in spite of your father's great service to medicine and the University here in Budapest? We just thank god that so far we have been spared their fate. We know that the knock on the door could still come at any moment – we know that we are not out of danger just because the Soviets have taken over the city – but in the meantime we are doing all we can to help as many of our brethren who are still here and in need.'

When they had finished the meal, Hanneke presented Eszter with a large bag full of fresh food and milk for her to take home for herself and Eva. Claussen asked her to return at midday the next day and they wished her a safe journey home.

Eva walked back up the road with a light step, as if she had just been the recipient of a miracle.

CHAPTER 28

The war in Europe was over, following the suicide of Adolf Hitler and the German unconditional surrender on 8 May 1945. Peter settled down to life with his mother in the farm that she had occupied with his father. Nobody had come back to claim it – the original owners were presumed dead in the war and after the death of his father his mother handed the farm over to her son. He took over most of the work, including the rearing and milking of the cows, leaving his mother to continue the less onerous work of looking after the farmhouse, the care of the hens and collecting the eggs once a day.

Now that the Germans had been defeated, and the camps at Auschwitz and Birkenau lay deserted, there was no requirement to supply what produce the farm had to the German invaders. Peter was able to start delivering milk, eggs and chickens by the horse and cart previously used by his father to the markets that were slowly coming back to life in nearby towns. The cows were doing well and the milk yield increasing; in time he was able to afford to buy in more animals so that after a few years they had a herd of some twenty cows. In the same way, a point was also reached where he was also able to keep some of the milk and cream back so that he could start making it into cheese. He had never done this before, but his mother was able to guide him how best to proceed and he was pleased with the results he was starting to achieve.

Now that he was in charge of the farm, Peter applied for and was granted legal ownership of the farm and its estate by reason of unchallenged occupancy. There was not a large amount of land attached to the farm, but there were a couple of fields which had hitherto lain fallow. The old horse his parents had inherited with the farm eventually died, but after a year he had saved enough money from the dairy produce he had sold to buy himself another horse, harnesses and ploughing equipment. He ploughed one of the fields and planted wheat the next spring and, when that produced a reasonable harvest in August, he did the same with the other field the next year. He knew enough about farming to know that it could be a tenuous living, dependent on the vagaries of the weather and what it might throw at them. He calculated that it would be best to continue down the line of mixed farming, to increase the income he could achieve, but that it would also be insurance for the bad times as well as the good. This decision was justified after only three years, when a sweltering hot summer and a good harvest was followed by a summer of heavy rain which severely damaged the crops. The harvest was not completely ruined, but the yield was much reduced and the quality of the wheat obtained generally rather poor that year. Their income over the year was significantly lower, but was at least fortified by the increasing money that was being brought in from the dairy business.

* * *

One day in the summer of 1948 Peter looked through the window and saw a man he did not recognise marching up the garden path. There was a rap on the door. Peter opened the door hesitantly. The man who was standing in front of him appeared to be wearing some sort of uniform he did not recognise: with a green shirt and a red tie.

'Can I help you, Sir?' Peter asked, embarrassed by his subservience as soon as he had spoken. Why should he feel like this on his own property? But he'd had a premonition about why the man was there.

'I represent the Central Committee of the Polish Workers' Party and it is my responsibility to carry out the plan to collectivize all Polish farms in this area of southern Poland. The decision to restructure Polish agriculture has been taken to protect small farmers from ownership by the rich kulaks who have been decreed as village capitalists and who are thereby exploiting other peasants.'

'Please come in,' Peter said, opening the door widely to the man and trying not to show his fear at what might be about to happen to his farm and his livelihood.

Over the next hour Peter sat explaining to the officer every detail of the small farm's modest size and meagre earnings. The man sat in front of him making detailed notes and interrogating him about every aspect of the farm. After he finished the interrogation, he walked outside with Peter to conduct an inspection of the farm. This didn't take long, there being only two fields and one horse to inspect. The man counted all the cows, even though Peter had already told him how many he had.

When the inspection had finished, Peter walked with the man back to the gate and stood there anxiously waiting to hear what the decision about the fate of his farm was to be. He already knew of farms not much bigger than his that had already been taken into collectives, essentially being requisitioned by the state with the loss of control and earnings for the farmer that this entailed. The man stood for a long time reading through his notes before he gave his decision.

'Since you have less than eight hectares and only one horse you will not be registered as a kulak and taken into the state collective at this time,' the man finally announced his decree. 'But we shall continue to monitor the farm on an annual basis,' the man said, his eyes piercing into Peter as if he had been guilty of some misdemeanour, 'and have the right to reverse this decision at any time should the situation change.

'For generations the kulaks have farmed the lands for their own selfish reasons, using and abusing their peasant labourers for their own ends. The time has now come for the common land to be used in the interest of the common good.'

Having delivered this parting lecture, the man turned on his heel, opened the gate and marched back up the road without even being civil enough to say goodbye. Peter realised that the man had not even given him his name either.

Peter stood at the gate looking after the officious representative. He had been given a reprieve of sorts, but knew that this might only be temporary and that his ability to develop his farm into a much larger thriving business over the next few years had been dealt a serious blow.

* * *

All this time Peter had not forgotten Eszter. His love for her had not in any way diminished. He carried with him the on-going hope that one day she would re-appear looking for him. But as time went by he had to tell himself quietly that this was less and less likely. After a number of years he knew he had to accept the fact that Eszter had had no choice but to continue her life with her husband Robert and daughter Eva, in addition to any more children they might now have produced. From time to time he had felt the urge to leave the farm and travel back to Budapest to seek her out once more. But each time this urge came upon him, he sublimated it in the knowledge that such a visit was likely to be sure to fail and therefore to be unbearably humiliating. In spite of his unremitting love for the girl, he was also too proud to put himself in this position.

CHAPTER 29

August, 1945

R obert never came back. After he had stormed out one evening, no doubt to get drunk yet again, Eszter woke early the next morning surprised to find that her drunken husband was not in the bed next to her, snoring loudly and with his breath reeking of stale alcohol from the night before, as was usually the case. Indeed, on more than one occasion recently, she had been woken in the middle of the night with Robert having a seizure in the bed next to her, swamping the bed linen and mattress with urine in his incontinence as he fitted. On those occasions she had been frightened – not only because the episodes made her realise that her husband's alcoholism had reached the low point where it was threatening his very life but also for the safety of herself and her young daughter when he was in this state. She did not know what the prospect of their life alone would be should he die during one of these seizures, even though Robert had never been any help or support to them when he was sober. She had fully accepted the fact that their relationship had ended and was beyond repair. But more worrying to her was the fear about the unknown lonely future she and Eva were surely facing again before long. She missed the family she had lost in Auschwitz more than ever.

Eszter had heard nothing at all from Peter since he left her the day Robert re-appeared in her life. She hoped that he was alive and well, perhaps back in Poland with his family. She could not help wishing that he would get news to her one day, if only to let her know that he was safe and well. But as time went on she began to feel confused about his lack of communication. She could not understand why, having professed his deep love for her, he could carry on with a new life and leave her behind so irrevocably. After a number of years with no communication whatever from Peter, however, she reached the point where she knew she had to accept that he had moved on with his life, most likely with another woman.

Eva was growing fast now, exploring independently and starting to ask lots of questions, just like any toddler of her age. Eszter tried to explain to her daughter the reason for her father's absence; at the same time she also did not let her forget the time that Peter was with them, and talked about him frequently. She refused to use the epithet 'uncle' before his name, and as Eva grew older she would quite often come out with questions to her, such as: 'Mummy, what do you think Peter is doing now?' Eszter realised that the child had understood that mention of his name was something that was pleasing to her mother, and Eszter could not help but take comfort from these interchanges.

About three months after Peter had left, Eszter was lying in bed one night, unable to get to sleep, as was often the case since Peter had gone. Reflecting on the recent events of her life, it suddenly occurred to her that she had not had a period since Peter's departure. The next morning she awoke feeling sick. She realised immediately that she was pregnant.

CHAPTER 30

September, 1945

A	rno and his wife sat at the table in their living room eating breakfast. Their friend Raoul Wallenberg had been missing since shortly after the Soviets captured Budapest from the Germans in January. Nothing had been heard from him since. It was rumoured that he may have fled back to Sweden, but there were also stories that he had been arrested by the Soviets and taken to Moscow and perhaps imprisoned there. They had feared for their own safety since then, in the uncertainty of life under Soviet rule. In spite of this, Claussen continued carrying on with his normal working day, as if there was nothing unusual. He had a number of clients booked in to see him that morning.

There was a soft tap on their front door. Arno and Hanneke looked at each other. They were not expecting any callers at this hour of the morning; it was more than an hour before Arno's first client was due. He got up and went to the door, peering through the spy hole before he opened it. As far as he could see there was nobody standing on the other side. He unbolted the door and very cautiously opened it a crack and looked out. Standing on the step was Hans, the small boy he and his contacts continued to use to pass messages between each other. Claussen smiled to himself. He ought to have a spy hole lower down the door to check for visiting children.

'Message from Mr Wallenberg,' Hans said in his chiming voice, passing a letter through the crack in the door.

'Thank you Hans, you're a good boy,' Arno said, amazed by the news. The boy beamed at him and turned and ran off down the street.

Claussen closed and locked the door again quickly and brought the sealed envelope back to the table; he sat down and sliced it open with a table knife.

'Need to speak urgently. Come to usual place. R,' was all that the enigmatic note said.

'What is it, dear?' his wife Hanneke asked, looking up at him.

'A message from Raoul! He's alive! It says he wants to meet up with me. Perhaps he has been in hiding in the city all this time, in spite of the rumours that the Soviets had arrested him in January. Or, if they did arrest him, perhaps he has now finally been released?'

Claussen turned the envelope over, examining it carefully. During their time working together Wallenberg had always used different stationery with each message he sent, and Arno had no reason to think that this envelope was different from the others Wallenberg had used in the past. He examined the note paper more carefully: it did not look quite the same as any of the paper that had been used for messages to him before. Sometimes these had been on official Swedish legation headed writing paper, presumably to give the bearer some authority if intercepted, and at other times on different types of official or legal looking notepaper. This letter was typed on cheap plain lined paper and came in a brown business envelope. But he decided that either changing the format again must be part of the ploy Wallenberg was still using to avoid suspicion, or simply due to the fact that, wherever he was now, he did not have access to any official notepaper.

'Raoul wants to see me straight away,' he said to Hanneke. 'He doesn't say what it's about, except that it's urgent. I better go now.'

He left his breakfast unfinished, pulled on his coat and hat and tucked his briefcase under his arm, as he always did when he went out of the house on legal business. He bent down and kissed his wife on the cheek. 'Apologise to my client and ask him to wait if he arrives before I get back,' he said as he placed his hat on his head and left the house.

'Do be careful, Arno,' Hanneke said to him as he went out of the door.

Arno looked at his watch as he walked down the street. It was only just after seven thirty a.m. He walked up Andrassy Avenue, making his way north towards the Swedish legation office in Budapest. Previously they had met as rarely as possible in person, usually communicating by clandestine messages. When they did have the need to talk, they would meet on one of the park benches in a small square off the main part of Andrassy Avenue behind the legation. Arno was making his way there now. Whatever the reason Raoul wanted to meet up with him again after not having made contact for months, he knew there must be a very urgent reason why he needed to speak to him now in person, otherwise he would have chosen an hour of the day when other people were coming and going, as he usually had done in the past. It was easier to be to be less conspicuous when they were part of a crowded park, two men sitting on a bench talking together.

Claussen crossed the Oktogon interchange and walked on up Andrassy Avenue towards where the embassy buildings were mostly situated. At this point of the war, with the Russian invasion of Hungary and the city under Soviet occupation, all of the foreign consulates were still shut down. Those buildings which had been taken over by the Nazis for their own use were now locked and boarded up or had been occupied by the Soviets to use themselves. A hundred metres from the Swedish legation office, he turned off Andrassy into a side street which led to the small park they used as their rendezvous point.

As he came to the end of the side street, Arno came to a sudden halt. In front of him was something he was certainly not expecting. The usually quiet square was teeming with Soviet army personnel and military vehicles. In that instant, he had to decide whether to walk on as nonchalantly as he could into and across the park, or take evasive action and leave the scene.

As slowly as he could, Claussen turned round and started to stroll back down the street he had come from, tapping his fingers on his forehead and throwing his open hand into the air, pretending to be a man who had forgotten something. A few brief seconds later he realised immediately that he had made the wrong decision.

'Halt!' shouts rang out behind him. He could hear the sound of running boots chasing after him. Not looking back, he quickened his step without actually breaking into a run and turned left into a small alleyway that he knew was a short cut back to the Oktogon interchange. The sound of the boots of soldiers running after him seemed to have dissolved. But as he neared the end of the alleyway three Soviet soldiers ran into view right in front of him. They stopped in unison and stood in a line across the road, raising their rifles to their faces in his direction as they did so. He realised at once that he had been ambushed. He turned slowly to look behind him. There was another line of soldiers across the alleyway he had just entered, also with their raised guns pointing towards him. Arno turned again to face the three soldiers in front of him, raising his right arm above his head, meaning as if to make a gesture of welcome. As he did so, the last thing he heard was a rifle crack. He fell backwards and landed on his back on the street. His body lay there dead with bright red blood oozing from a single bullet hole in his forehead.

CHAPTER 31

September, 1945

Four months after Robert had left her, Eszter was still living alone with Eva in her parents' apartment in Budapest. While it was a relief to be free of the drunkenness and animosity that her husband had shown to her – and she hoped fervently for that reason that he never came back – she was lonely on her own. She still bore a hope that Peter might someday re-appear. She saw Hanna most days, either in the courtyard outside or passing in the street. And Hanna would always stop to ask her how she was and be supportive.

Eszter had no doubt by now that she was indeed pregnant. The sickness had settled down, but her periods had not re-appeared and her breasts were uncomfortable and felt heavier than usual. She lay awake at night trying to work out whether the father of her unborn child was Peter or Robert, but she could not know for sure. She realised that it could be either of them – that she might have no idea even after the child was born – but she prayed that it will have been Peter's child. Even if she never got to see him again, she would find comfort in the knowledge that she might be bearing his baby, might have his child to bring up, even if she could not have him. She was frightened about how she would manage the birth on her own, and her fear increased slowly inside her – as did the child – as the weeks went by. In spite of her concerns, she did not feel able to confide in Hanna. Not yet. But she knew that she would have to as her time drew near. She was going to need help during her confinement.

One morning Eszter was walking back from the market at the end of the street, holding Eva's hand in one hand and a bag of greens in another. In spite of the windfall she had inherited from her father, there was barely any bread to be found in the city, let alone meat or other foods. But she knew she must do her best to eat some vegetables at least every day for the sake of her unborn child. Eva was crying that she was hungry – had started to do so regularly in the last few weeks – and this made Eszter even more desperate about the situation they found themselves in.

As they crossed the road at the corner or their street, Eszter bent down to lift Eva by her arm to step up the high stone curb on the other side. As she did so, Eva swung herself forward, wanting to play her favourite swinging game, and landed hard up the kerb, taking her mother down with her. Eszter fell heavily forwards onto the cobbles. Immediately she experienced a deep, searing pain through her lower abdomen. As she lay there in the road dazed she felt a rush of fluid pouring out of her from between her legs; vaguely she was aware of dark red blood pooling around her where she lay. She was floating in and out of consciousness; the pain was intense, coming in waves that she could not stop. She heard Eva screaming next to her, but her vision was blurred and she could not see where her daughter was. She was not able to speak to reassure her little girl. She had hardly enough breath for herself.

After only a few minutes Hanna appeared by chance, running towards mother and child lying there on the cobbled roadside.

'My God, Eszter! What's happened?!' she cried. Eszter was in too much pain to speak to her neighbour, but Hanna realised at once what the problems was. She saw the pool of dark blood oozing round Eszter as she lay there and could see that she was writhing in abdominal pain. She took little Eva by her hand and sat her firmly on the curb side, a few metres away from where Eszter was lying.

'Sit there like a good girl, while I help mummy up,' she said. Then, very gently, she put her arms around Eszter and drew her up to a near-standing position.

'Let's take mummy home, Eva,' Hanna said to the little girl, as she gently started to drag Eszter backwards towards the front door of the building, which was luckily no more than about thirty metres away. As she reached up to turn the knob on the large front door, she looked over her shoulder to see with relief that little Eva was obediently following her closely behind.

Once they were inside the door and at the entrance to their courtyard, Hanna stopped for breath before continuing. Eszter was a dead weight in her arms, falling in and out of consciousness and unable to stand without Hanna's help, let alone to walk. Hanna more or less dragged Eszter across the courtyard and through the front door of her apartment, across the living room into the bedroom, and deposited Eszter face down on her bed. She went back to shut the door behind Eva who had followed them through, then went to the tap to fetch a wet cloth. Slowly, she turned Eszter onto her back. Her face was deathly white and wet with cold sweat; she had obviously lost a great deal of blood. She was also contorted in pain. Hanna bathed the sweat from her face then, with the gentle hands of a nurse, she removed Eszter's clothes, one by one, being as careful as she could to cause her the minimum pain as she rolled her back and forth across the bed. Once she had done so, she started on the task of cleaning up the blood and birth fluid that was still leaking, although now more slowly, from between Eszter's legs. She cleaned the dry blood and amniotic fluid from Eszter's thighs. Last of all, she picked up the aborted dead foetus that was lying in the bed, and tenderly placed it in a paper bag which she then lowered into the refuse bin outside in the courtyard.

CHAPTER 32

March, 1946

The nearby town of Rajsko was his favourite place to go to market. Peter would load his horse and cart with whatever produce he had to sell and head off to spend the day there. That morning, he spent a few hours doing business, selling the produce and any animals he wanted to get rid of, buying in a couple of chickens or a goat in return. Once he had completed all the business he needed to, he headed for the bar in the market which was his regular place for a lunch break.

'Hello, Peter. How are you today?' Julia smiled up at him. She was the youngest daughter of Anna, the woman who owned the bar, and was usually there helping her mother out. Julia was blonde and blue-eyed and quite attractive. She had obviously taken a liking to Peter, and did not hide the fact. For his part, Peter continued to compare any woman he met against his memories of his love for Eszter. But he had to admit to himself on that sunny May morning that it was nice to meet someone who was as warm towards him as the weather.

'I'm well, thanks, Julia,' Peter replied. 'What's been happening to you since I last saw you?'

Julia dropped the cloth she was cleaning the counter with and sat with her elbows on the counter, her face in her hands, ignoring the other customers while she gave him her sole attention.

'Oh, not very much has happened since I last saw you,' she said. 'Business here has been as steady as always. How're things on the farm?'

'I'm very busy,' Peter replied. 'In fact, with three of the cows calving and the two fields needing planting, I've been run off my feet. I was thinking yesterday that I could do with a farm hand, but I cannot afford to employ one.'

'Could I come up and help you?' Julia said immediately and with enthusiasm. 'My mother really doesn't need me here at the moment – she can manage. And to tell you the truth I could do with a break from the boredom of this place. It would do me good to get away for a bit, to have a bit of fresh air out on a farm!'

Peter was taken by surprise by her unexpected offer. He replied slowly, thinking as he spoke. 'As a matter of fact, that would be helpful. As long as your mother agrees,' he said as an afterthought.

Julia arrived at the farm two days later. She left the small case containing her belongings in the living room and went straight out with Peter onto the farm without asking him where she would be accommodated while she was there helping him out. After he had shown her around the small farm, they went back to the farmhouse and sat down together in the living room.

'What are the main things I can help you with, Peter?' she asked after he had told her how he ran things on the farm. Peter listed some of the most important things he needed help with immediately.

'Mother is very old now, and – although she wouldn't admit it – is having trouble coping with some of the tasks she has always been responsible for, things she has done without fail all her life, such as taking care of the chickens, cleaning out the shed and collecting the eggs.'

'I'll start with that, then,' Julia interrupted him, 'and perhaps, at the same time I could help your mother with some of the cleaning and cooking and other chores in the house?'

'Thank you Julia, that would be very helpful.' Peter could not hide his relief. In truth, the care of the farm and the farmhouse had been starting to bear down on him in recent months, and it had reached the point where he knew he really needed help from somebody he could trust. A fleeting thought occurred to him that Julia might have other motives for placing herself into his life and his gratitude. But at that moment he didn't really care. He did not doubt that she was genuine and sincere, even if she had developed a soft spot for him personally.

CHAPTER 33

May, 1946

It was exactly a year since the end of the war in Europe. Eszter had stayed on in Budapest with her daughter Eva in her parents' apartment near the basilica. Life was still hard, but at least the city and the whole of Europe were now living in relative peace. Eva was two years old now, and bright as a button, getting up to all sorts of mischief. Rationing was still in place and food and supplies in general still hard to come by in the markets. But things were improving very slowly and at least they were not starving any more. Eszter had used the money that Mr Claussen had passed on to her from her father carefully and there was still a sizeable amount remaining. When she did visit one of the money lenders to exchange a dollar note for Hungarian pengös, she always received a large amount in exchange. Foreign currency was like gold in Hungary, especially US dollars. She continued to give thanks to her father every day for having saved them in this way.

It occurred to Eszter, on the first anniversary of the war's ending, that she had heard nothing from Arno Claussen since the day she had last visited him to collect the money he had been keeping for her. That must have been nine months ago. She felt a little guilty about the fact that she had not taken the trouble to call on the Claussens again, at least to pass by to repeat her grateful thanks to them and wish them well. But time had flown by and she seemed to have been so busy looking after herself and Eva. She decided that she should make amends and pay them a visit.

She left Eva playing with Hanna for a while and walked to number sixteen Paulay Ede Street. When she got there she saw that the sign announcing 'Claussen & Groenwold, Attorneys at Law' was still on the wall. She rang the bell.

The door was opened by a man she hadn't met before. He had whiskers down each side of his face and a moustache that was curled up at the corners of his mouth, as well as a maroon waistcoat. He was obviously another lawyer. 'Can I help you madam?' he said politely to her.

'My name's Eszter, I've come to pay Mr Claussen a visit. Is he at home?

The man paused, then opened the door to her. 'Won't you come in, please,' he said.

Eszter walked in to the office and sat down at the large lawyer's desk, the same place she had sat when she came to visit Arno Claussen on her previous visit. The man sat on the other side of the desk.

'I'm Max Groenwold, Arno Claussen's partner in law,' he explained. 'I'm sorry to tell you, but Arno was shot by the Russians last September. He had been lured by a false message to a rendezvous near to the Swedish legation off Andrassy Avenue. He tried to retreat when he saw the Russian soldiers gathered there, but was ambushed in an alley close by and shot in the head.'

'Oh, no!' Eszter cried. 'That is terrible. I'm so sorry. I feel so guilty that it has taken me so long to try and make contact with Arno and Hanneke again. I only passed by to express my thanks to them for the kindness they showed to me last year. They saved me and my daughter from starvation. I should have come to visit them up again much sooner. How is Hanneke, is she still safe and well?'

'Immediately after Arno was shot, the Russians came and searched the house here, probably looking for evidence of Arno's collaboration with the Swedish diplomat Raoul Wallenberg. They ransacked the place, but eventually left having found nothing to interest them. Shortly after that, Hanneke fled. I understand she is now living with her sister in Pecs,' Groenwold said.

'Oh, God,' Eszter moaned, her face in her handkerchief. 'I'm so sad for them. They were such good people. I am so sorry that it has taken me so long to come back visit them to thank them for what they did for me.'

'It would not have made any difference,' Max Groenwold comforted her. Arno was shot very shortly after you had been to see them. It was lucky that you were not caught up in the trap as well.'

'How did the Russians get to find out about Arno and his involvement with Mr Wallenberg? Why should they have objected to the fact that he had been working to protect Jewish families from arrest and death?'

. 'We don't know for sure. But it turned out that they had apprehended the small boy Hans, who was the message carrier between the members of the group of us trying to rescue Hungarian Jews. Under the threat of beatings, they then used Hans to carry a message to Arno to entice him to the square behind the Swedish legation that day. After they had used him in this way, poor Hans was also shot dead himself later the same day.

'In January last year, very soon after the Soviets finally entered Budapest after their two month long siege, our friend Raoul Wallenberg, the Swedish diplomat, went missing without trace. There were rumours that he had been shot – although we could find no witnesses who might have confirmed this – or that he had been arrested and transported away to Moscow, along with his Hungarian driver. Either way, nothing has been heard from him since – our lines of secret communication do not stretch as far as Moscow! – but we fear that Wallenberg too has been 'eliminated'. We only assume that because of the rumours that went round at the time and the fact that he too disappeared he from the face of the earth. Arno seems to have been caught up in the Soviets purge of all those associated with Wallenberg, probably to eliminate them before they could tell the world about Raoul's disappearance. I was also involved with Raoul and Arno in the project to save the Jewish people of Hungary from mass murder. I'm sorry to say I am now one of only a few of us to have survived the war to tell the story of what was achieved.'

After such shocking news, Eva took a little time to compose herself. When she had done so, she bade Max goodbye and walked very sadly home.

CHAPTER 34

June, 1946

Life on the farm became considerably easier for Peter with Julia helping him. He could be out in the fields all day – or off to market till late, returning not long before dusk – with the knowledge that Julia was seeing to all the other chores that needed to be done. In addition to that, it was a comfort to him to know that there was someone around to keep his mother company when he was away from the farmhouse; and the two women seemed to get on well.

One Wednesday in June he took the horse and cart off to Rajsko for his usual weekly visit to the market. After he had completed his business selling the produce he had brought to the market, he spent a couple of hours sitting having a beer with Joel, another farmer about his age who he had become particularly friendly with. When he arrived back at the farmhouse later than usual, the light was fading.

As soon as he had tied up his horse and walked up the path, the farmhouse door flew open and Julia stood there in front of him, 'Peter,' she whispered, 'come in,' She reached out for his hand and led him into the living room.

'What is it, Julia?' Peter asked at once, sensing that something was wrong.

'It's your mother, Peter. Irena is dead.' They sat on the bench in front of the stove and she took his hand gently once more. 'I came in from cleaning out the hens about two hours ago. I made her some tea, and took it in to her bedroom where she had gone to have her afternoon nap. As soon as I saw her, I knew. She was lying in the bed peacefully, at rest. Peter, I'm so sorry.'

Peter rose to his feet and walked in to his mother's bedroom. The room she had shared with Artur for all the years of their marriage. Julia had pulled the sheet up to her chin, but not over her face. He looked at her white, sunken face, the face of an old woman, which was not how he wished to remember her, but could see that she was at rest. Her features were of someone who had died peacefully.

The next day Peter buried his mother in a grave which he dug outside the back of the farmhouse, to lay her to rest next to her husband Artur. He prepared a wooden cross with her name carved upon it, identical to that which he had placed on the grave of his father a year before. He had no religion, or rather any religion he'd had had been destroyed during his time spent as a guard at Birkenau. He could not believe in a god after the horrors he had witnessed there. But he still had a faith of sorts. He had faith that his parents had brought him up to love life – however much he still could not accept or explain the things he had witnessed – and he knew they had loved him and that he'd loved them for what they were to him.

As he stood by the two graves, Peter thought back on both of his parents' lives. They were honest and brave people. They had stood by each other all those years, never wavering in their love for each other. Of all the trials of life they had endured, their life together during the German occupation and war years must have been the hardest to endure. They may not have had to suffer the physical attacks and degradation that all those poor people he had witnessed in Auschwitz-Birkenau had. But they had survived the loss of their family home in Brzezinka, a place where generations of the Leahy family had lived before them. And they'd managed to flee from the place before it was razed to the ground. Yes, this had happened because of a chance conversation that Artur had overheard the day before the place was to be evacuated by force. But having dragged themselves clear of the danger, they had been very courageous to sit out the rest of the war in the farm they had taken over so near to the Nazi occupied death camp, knowing the danger that it represented to themselves. Last but not least, they had lost two of their three precious sons during the war and never let this be a reason for discarding their courage in life.

There was no one else present at his mother's graveside, just himself and Julia. He would not have wanted a priest, even if there was one in the area, which there was not. Julia stood next to him, side by side, and as she did so she took him by the hand for a second time. He could see that there were tears running down her cheeks too. He knew she had become very fond of Irena. He said a few words to the skies, proclaiming his love for his mother and thanking both his parents for caring for him. They both hung their heads, still holding hands, deep in their own thoughts for some minutes. Peter then stepped forward and with a spade started to shovel the earth into the grave that he had dug for his mother. They had no coffin, but Julia had wrapped her in a plain blanket and he had carried her tenderly from the farmhouse and laid her in the bottom of the grave. Slowly, with each shovelful that he covered her body with, he mouthed a quiet prayer to her. After he had finished, he placed the cross into the earth and hammered it down with the back of his spade.

As he stood up he turned to Julia. She placed her arms around his neck to console him and lay her head on his shoulder. Peter bent down and kissed her on the lips.

CHAPTER 35

About three months after his mother's death Peter and Julia were married. They took themselves to the town hall in Rajsko on a market day afternoon and were wed by the mayor in a brief civil ceremony. The only other people there were his friend Joel, whom he had invited as his witness, and Julia's mother, Anna. Afterwards, they made for the bar in the market and celebrated with some simple food and a few beers. The couple returned happily to the farm which Peter had now inherited from his parents.

Peter had not lost his love for Eszter. Before he proposed marriage to Julia he had told himself that he was not taking her as his bride as a substitute for her. But he had come to accept, with the inevitable passage of time, that life does move on and we all have to move with it. In his own way, therefore, he had come to love Julia without relinquishing his love for Eszter. He was peaceful in that knowledge. Ever since he first met Julia he had talked openly about Eszter. Julia was well aware of his continuing love for this other woman, and even knew the details of how they had met at the railhead to Birkenau concentration camp. But she did not seem to be bothered by the fact. She was an optimistic young woman who was keen to live for the future and not worry about the past.

Another year had passed and another harvest finished. Julia gave birth to a son whom they called Aleksy and the next year to a daughter whom they called Greta. Peter and Julia lived on in relative peace on the farm, despite the many economic and political hardships of the time. Twenty years later their son Aleksy married a local farmer's daughter called Iren and they set up home near to Peter and Julia.

CHAPTER 36

1952

L ife in Budapest for Eszter in the years after the end of the war was far from easy. The city was dreary and grey, the only colour to be seen came from the red flags and red stars placed on top of all large buildings; a flower bed in front of the chain bridge planted with red flowers in the shape of a hammer and sickle was hardly a relief from the otherwise greyness to be seen and felt all around the place. Hungary had become an authoritarian communist state under its leader Matyas Rákosi. The security police were undertaking purges to eliminate all those opposed to Rákosi's leadership. Thousands of people were re-located to release housing for those who were members of the Working People's Party, resulting in a shortage of housing for those non-party members that were left. Many other thousands were arrested, in a policy aimed at removing the perceived threat of the intellectual and bourgeois classes, and tortured, tried and imprisoned in concentration camps – where they experienced terrible living conditions and malnutrition – or deported and interned as slave labour on collective farms to the east where many died or were executed.

Under Rákosi, Hungary's government had become one of the most repressive in Europe. The educational system was politicised to supplant the educated classes with a 'toiling intelligentsia'. Russian language study and Communist political instruction were made mandatory in schools and universities nationwide. Religious schools were nationalized and church leaders were replaced by those loyal to the government. In 1949 the leader of the Hungarian Catholic Church, Cardinal József Mindszenty, who had openly opposed communism and the communist persecution in his country, was arrested and sentenced in a show trial to life imprisonment on fake charges of espionage. There were chronic shortages in basic foodstuffs resulting in rationing of bread, sugar, flour and meat. All this, in addition to the fact that jobs and housing were very difficult to obtain had a cumulative negative effect on the people of Budapest and fuelled discontent among them and the population of the country at large.

Eva was eight years old now. She was doing well at junior school and Eszter did all she could to support her daughter in her education, knowing how important this would be for her future life. Eszter looked around to find Eva a middle school which would suit both her and her daughter. Eventually she came across a school which was situated conveniently not very far from their apartment in the Pest district of Budapest. Eva could walk to school from home, and Eszter would accompany her daughter to and from school every day. In addition to its convenient situation, Eszter had chosen this school for Eva because she liked its sense of community. On the first visit she had made to the school, an open evening for prospective parents, she had found all the staff open and very friendly. They were clearly all working as one team committed to the school's philosophy of an education for their pupils which didn't just mean 'learning'. There was a healthy emphasis on character development, team working and the growth of children into young adults fit for their lives in the future.

Most of all, Eszter was reassured by the fact that not once during that evening did she hear a member of the staff preach the communist 'mantra' to prospective parents. She knew from having visited other schools that they had all been forced to follow the Party line in educating their children, more likely from a fear of what would be the consequences rather than a belief in the system that was being imposed upon them. No doubt communist political instruction was on the curriculum somewhere in this school too, ready to impress the communist inspectors whenever they should visit. But not one word of it was mentioned that evening. The mandatory pictures of Joseph Stalin could be found hanging in all large buildings and schools in the city, in the post office and other civic buildings and were carried in Mayday parades. Although this school was no exception in having to exhibit Stalin's portrait as well, Eszter noted that his picture had been placed in a less prominent alcove at the end of the entrance hall.

This school's ethos very much came down from the headmistress, Kitti Pasztor, who spoke so well from the stage about her team's ambitions for nurturing the young children in their care. Not once did the headmistress make any reference to her own political views – because it would not have been safe for her to do so – but Eszter could sense that she was liberal, caring and against the political tide. When Eszter met the head one to one she really took to her and found her a very engaging person, one she felt she would like as a personal friend. She was flattered when Kitti asked if she would join one of her parents' advice groups. Kitti was really keen for all parents to engage in and contribute to the development of the school's future. Eszter accepted at once.

Eszter's involvement with the school's parents' group meant that she was now going out to various meetings often two or three evenings a week – leaving Eva at home to do her homework. She was really enjoying this opportunity to get to meet people and make friends. She met a lot of interesting people on these evenings out. The other parents came from many different backgrounds, with all sorts of jobs and professions. They never spoke openly about their lives in Hungary under the Soviet rule, but Eszter knew that most of them, like her, had been scarred by the war and now were being scarred in turn by the political oppression which had replaced it. She avoided talking to any of these new friends about her own horrific wartime experiences, and she was aware that in general they were also reticent to talk about their own personal histories, wanting to put the war behind them and move on to a new life in this new decade in spite of the Soviet repression they were all now living under.

In addition to the meetings held at the school, Eszter was now meeting up socially with a small group of half a dozen or so of the parents that she had become particularly friendly with. They would spend their evenings in each other's apartments and she had invited her friends to visit her in her apartment one evening. From time to time, they would meet up to go to a music concert which took to their liking. While there was still a lot of remaining post-war poverty and economic recession in Hungary, music life in Budapest was getting back on its feet, with regular concerts now appearing on the calendar.

She was not the only parent in her group who was a single mother. There were quite a number of them, women who had lost their husbands and partners as a result of fighting in the war or because of the war. Her closest friend Lotti had lost her husband when the house they were living in had been destroyed by a bombing raid one night. Lotti and her daughter Zoe, who was Eva's age and had become very friendly with Eva, had survived, but her husband had been crushed to death by the falling debris as the house collapsed around them. Lotti and her daughter had been re-housed in Eszter's building in a flat one floor up from them. So now not only were the two girls great friends, Eva and Lotti would pop up or down to see each other almost every day.

The only single father was a man called Tamas. He had also lost his wife in a raid on the street – she had been caught in the cross fire during a flare up of street fighting during the Soviet invasion of Budapest. She had died in his arms to the entrance to their building as he tried to pull her inside the door to safety, Tamas had told her. Tamas was not only a parent but he was also a teacher at the school. Not unreasonably, he also took the opportunity to join the parents' support group. Eszter had come to like him a lot. He had a great sense of humour and was fun to be with.

One Wednesday evening, when the group of parents was just winding up Tamas came to talk to Eszter.

'Eszter, I've managed to get a couple of tickets to see *Don Giovanni* at the Opera House on Saturday. I wondered if you would like to come with me?'

'That would be lovely, Tamas. I'd love to come.' In spite of the Soviet occupation, the Opera House had been rejuvenated since the war, not least by the conductor Otto Klemperer, who had been music director there for three years from 1947 to 1950. It was by now putting on a full season of opera every year.

'Great,' said Tamas. How about we meet in the foyer about 7 p.m.?'

The evening was a fantastic experience for Eszter. It was in fact the first time she had ever seen a live opera performance, let alone been inside the impressive neo-Renaissance Budapest Opera House building. The Opera House dated back to the 1880s, when its construction had been part funded by the Emperor Franz-Joseph I of Austria-Hungary. Sitting there in a favoured seat, Eva was in awe of her surroundings but even more so of the excellence of the singers, orchestra and lavish costumes and sets. She enjoyed the whole outing no end. She told Tamas so, and thanked him very much for taking her as she waved him goodbye.

A few weeks later Tamas came over to her at the end of one of their parents' evenings to say he had obtained two more seats at the opera, this time to see *The Magic Flute*. Eszter jumped at the invitation to accompany him again and had another very enjoyable evening once more. After the performance they did not go their separate ways straight home this time.

'How about we stop for a drink?' Tamas suggested to her. 'I know a nice place around the corner here.' He guided her to small café near the Opera House. When they got inside the place he had chosen they found themselves a table and he went off to fetch drinks.

Tamas came back with two glasses of wine and placed them on the table.

'There's something I've been wanting to ask you Eszter,' he said as he sat down next to her.

'Yes?' she said, sipping her wine. 'Go ahead.'

'I was wondering if you would say yes if I asked you to marry me?'

There was a pause as Eszter digested the question. She was taken aback. She suddenly saw that she should have realised that this might have been on his mind, but until that moment she had seen their friendship as exactly that. She had certainly not been looking out for a new romantic attachment. She did not know what to say. She liked the man very much, and didn't want to upset him.

'That is something that I have never considered, Tamas,' she said finally. I like you very much as a friend – a very good friend – but I am still deeply in love with another man. I hope this news doesn't upset you too much?'

'I understand, Eszter. I just wanted to let you know how I feel about you. I think we could make a very happy life together.' If he was feeling crestfallen he made a good attempt at not showing it, Eva thought to herself. She smiled at him and started to talk about the performance they had just seen, changing the subject to mask her embarrassment.

They had another glass of wine together and then Tamas escorted Eva back to her apartment. When they arrived at the front door to her building, he kissed her on the cheek and waved goodnight to her as he walked off up the road.

Eszter opened her front door and went to check on Eva. She had fallen asleep in the chair with a school book on her lap. Eszter placed the book on the table and gently carried her daughter to bed.

She went back and sat in the same chair in the living room. She had been quite unprepared for Tamas's proposal of marriage. Indeed, she still felt quite shocked by what had happened. She didn't blame him. She meant what she had told him: she liked him a lot as a man and as a friend. Her shock was more because of the way the episode had brought her feelings for Peter flooding back. She still loved him so very much. She couldn't help it. Her memory of her love for him was still very painful, and what had taken place that evening had made the pain of their continued separation bubble right back up to the surface. She knew if she told anybody else – including her friend Lotti – about her feelings for a man she had not seen now for nearly a decade, they would not understand. But this did not change the fact of how she felt.

That night Eszter lay in bed determining her future life. She knew for certain now that she would never ever live with another man again, if she could not live with Peter.

CHAPTER 37

October, 1956

E szter sat with her neighbour Lotti, who had come down from her apartment upstairs to talk to her friend.

'I couldn't get out of the house yesterday,' Eszter said. 'The streets outside were completely blocked. There were thousands of students marching to the Parliament building. They said they were protesting about the Hungarian Peoples Republic the Soviets have declared and the policies which they have imposed on Hungary.'

'I saw them, I watched them from my balcony,' Lotti said. 'It seemed to be a perfectly peaceful demonstration, but there were police in large numbers watching the protesters. They were standing in large groups on every corner and there were trucks full of reserves down many of the side streets.'

'Did you listen to the radio last night?' Eszter asked her friend. 'The students have now occupied the radio station and announced on the air that they are broadcasting as Radio Free Europe in the name of the peoples' revolution against the Soviet take over.'

Both women had heard the rumours that were now sweeping through the city of an imminent invasion of Hungary by Soviet armies.

'I went down to the bakery earlier this morning,' Eszter said to her friend. 'Ildicko was just shutting up. She gave me her last loaf of bread, and told me she was closing the bakery. She has decided to get out of Budapest and leave Hungary for good. She would trust her luck, even if she lost her life in the process, she said. She has no family left and could not bear to live life here under Soviet rule, she told me. What shall we do, Lotti?'

'I hear that there is a train leaving Keleti station every morning at 1 a.m. for the Austrian border and Vienna,' Lotti told her. 'I think we should take a chance tonight, before it is too late. The Soviets have apparently closed the borders already, but they are surely not likely to blow up a train full of civilians, are they? Anyway, if the Soviet invasion does not materialise – or if it proves to be a token gesture – we can come back to Budapest at any time, can't we?'

Eszter sat looking at the small corn doll she was holding in her hand. She still kept it in her skirt pocket, and often took it out to look at it when she was feeling low. She had had no contact from Peter since he'd left her with Robert more than a decade ago, but since then she had continued to wait for him, hoping that he might come back to find her one day. She knew that if he'd been there with her now he would have helped her make the decision whether she should leave her homeland or not. If her answer was 'yes', she knew he would help her escape, that he would go with her without hesitation. She decided that as soon as she had escaped Hungary, she would go looking for him in Poland. That was another reason to leave. To stop living her life alone any more without finding out once and for all what had happened to the only man she had really loved.

'Goodnight, then. See you at 1 a.m. In the meantime, I'm going to try and get some sleep.' Lotti left Eszter and went upstairs to her own apartment, where she had left her daughter Zoe sleeping. She apparently had no reservations that they had nothing to lose, and perhaps a lot to gain, in fleeing the city before the Soviets invaded.

Eszter sat on her own for a while, anxious about the fact that she might be putting her own life and Eva's in danger, but more than that excited that she had at last made the decision that she would leave Hungary and go in search of Peter. The fact that, once she had escaped to Austria she might have considerable difficulty travelling from there to Poland, which was already now part of the Soviet empire, did not deter her at that moment. She was determined to try. She smiled sheepishly at the thought that it had taken a political upheaval to make her brave enough to go in search of him, albeit it in a roundabout way, but excited that she had at last made a decision to go looking for him after all this time.

Having made her decision that leaving was the right thing to do, Eszter got up and left her apartment. She went downstairs to the basement flat where Hanna lived. She knocked on the door.

'Hello, Hanna,' Eszter said as soon as she opened the door to her. 'I hope I am not calling too late. I hope I haven't disturbed you?'

'No, you haven't' Hanna said, 'I was still up catching up with my mending.'

'That's good.' Eszter said. 'I've come to ask you a favour. I am planning to try and get on the train for Vienna in the early hours of the morning, taking Eva with me. There is a rumour that the Soviets are planning to invade the country imminently. I've been discussing the situation with Lotti and we have decided that it would be best to leave Budapest before they arrive. Once they have invaded Hungary, we will have no chance to leave and the country might be under Soviet domination for many years. We think it best to take our chance before this happens. I wonder whether you would be kind enough to keep an eye on my apartment while we are away?'

'Of course I'll look after the place,' Hanna said, taking the spare key Eszter was handing her. 'But are you sure it will be safe to attempt to leave Hungary? I heard on the wireless just now that the Soviets have already sealed the borders. What if they decide to stop people leaving by force? You could be shot!'

'I know there is a risk. But we've talked it over at length and think it is a risk worth taking. Wish us luck,' Eszter said as she left to get some belongings together to take with them on the journey.

As Eszter returned to her apartment she felt more uneasy having heard Hanna's concern. But it was too late for her to go back on her plan now.

CHAPTER 38

'Wake up, my Darling,' Eszter whispered quietly into her twelve-year old daughter Eva's ear, gently shaking her awake. 'We need to get up. We have a journey to go on. Be quiet, my Love. Don't ask questions. Just do as I say.' It was the night of 23ʳᵈ October, 1956, a date Eva would never forget. When she thought about that night in the future, Eva remembered being awoken by her mother at about 11 p.m. She had already been asleep for at least two hours. Her mother lifted her out of her bed and started pulling on her clothes, including her outdoor winter garments and her fur-lined hat, gloves and boots. Eszter gripped Eva's hand firmly and led her into the courtyard, locking the apartment door behind them and burying the key deeply in her inside pocket. She did not look back as they walked across the courtyard to the large front door and out of the building.

It was pitch black in the street; there were no street lights burning anywhere in the city. As they walked along the street they were joined by many others who were emerging from their houses like the silhouettes of ghosts in the darkness. Individuals and family groups; men, women and children, silently pressed in single file as near to the walls of the houses they passed as they could, making their way towards Keleti Station. Eszter walked determinedly away from their house, still gripping Eva's hand. As she walked, she straightened up on her tip toes from time to time, to look anxiously in front and behind her along the line of people, but could see no sign of her friend Lotti with her daughter Zoe. Eszter guessed that Lotti had decided not to chance it. In any case, Eszter thought to herself, I have made my decision for myself and Eva and there is no time to go back to see what has happened to Lotti and Zoe. If her friend had chosen to stay at the last minute, she prayed that they would be safe.

On arrival at the mainline station, they were ushered straight onto a train which was waiting and ready to go, its funnel bellowing out plumes of white steam. The train was already full, but the people on board were behaving politely, men helping others still arriving up the steep iron steps into the carriages. Having been hauled up roughly but kindly into one of the carriages, Eszter walked along the corridor carrying Eva in her arms looking for a compartment with enough space for them to fit in. Most of them were already very full. When she finally chose and entered a compartment which seemed a little less cramped than the others, the people inside moved over to accommodate the mother and her child as best as they could, without making any complaint.

A single long whistle sounded. Within no more than a minute the train pulled slowly out of the station, gaining speed as it left the outskirts of Budapest and headed westwards. By now, it was the early hours of the morning and Eva was dozing in and out of sleep as she lay on her mother's lap. 'Where are we going, Mama?' Eva asked her mother, waking up a little later to hear the sound of the train rattling over the rails as the journey progressed. 'Shush, my Darling, everything will be all right,' her mother replied. With this reassurance, Eva dozed off to sleep once more.

Only much later did Eva learn that they had been fleeing their home and city of Budapest before its occupation by the advancing Soviet army, who were imminently to subjugate the city and the whole of Hungary. In fear of the impending invasion of their country, some 200,000 Hungarians, including Eszter and her daughter Eva, were to flee prior to the arrival of the Soviet forces. It was 2 a.m. on 24 October, acting on orders from the Soviet Defence Minister Marshal Zhukov, that Russian tanks entered Budapest. As the Red Army throttled the anti-Soviet rebellion, the students who were occupying the radio station broadcast increasingly desperate pleas for help, pleas which were heard but ignored in the impotent west. The fighting which took place in the ensuing invasion resulted in the deaths of 2,500 Hungarians and 700 Soviet troops. It was a time of immense fear and apprehension for those Hungarians who had remained in the city and had not chosen to flee. Eszter and Eva were just one of thousands to have fled the city with literally an hour or two to spare. When she learned all this later, Eva was glad that her mother had kept the severity of the situation from her; she had not discussed with Eva at the time the mortal danger they were in.

Their train rumbled on west into the night past the city of Győr and onwards towards the Hungary-Austria border. About twenty minutes before reaching the border, an instruction came down through the train: 'Everybody lie flat on the floor and make no sound whatsoever!' Eszter pulled Eva onto the floor with her and they lay there sprawled face down for what seemed an age, almost too frightened to breathe, let alone to make any sound at all. The lights of the carriages had been switched off and the train approached the Austrian border slowly in silence. Eva remembered the sound of her mother's wrist watch next to her ear, ticking loudly as if it was counting down their fate.

After what seemed like eternity, the train passed through and cleared the bright floodlights of the Hungarian border, crossing without stopping and without challenge, apparently having been taken for an empty train returning to Vienna by the Soviet troops now occupying the Hungarian border post. All the adult passengers were well aware that, had their train been stopped and searched, they may not have survived to tell the tale. Eva would wonder in the future: 'Perhaps they knew, but chose to ignore our flight out of our motherland?' She had been spared much of the intense fear that her mother and the other adult passengers felt at the time. But she was able to understand it completely when their flight from Hungary was described to her in full when she was older by others who had been with them at the time.

After another long wait, the lights of the train were turned back on and the passengers who had been sprawled face down on the floor with their children and suitcases began to get up from where they had been frozen in fear and dust themselves down. While the occupants of the train were not outwardly celebrating, the atmosphere now was one of huge relief and a lightness of spirit. The mortal fear that the adults had been carrying with them during their flight from Budapest and the tension of their escape across the border had lifted. Within an hour the train was pulling into Vienna, a mood of excitement pervading the passengers. Eszter grasped Eva by the hand, jumped off the train with their bag and walked confidently down the platform. 'Come on, Poppet. We are free. This is the start of a new life!'

CHAPTER 39

Eszter and Eva walked out of the Hauptbahnhof station hand in hand, swinging their arms as they emerged from the shadow of the station concourse into the bright new day, dazzled by the low early morning sunshine. As Eszter stepped off the kerb into the road she looked up at the glittering light dancing in her eyes. Still holding her mother's hand, Eva was half a step behind her. In a flash, Eva caught the oncoming coach out of the corner of her left eye. The horses reared into the air, too late to avoid her mother, who was trampled into the road by their flaying hooves and dragged under the heavy carriage which they pulled behind them.

There must have been noise. There must have been shrieking and screaming. But Eva remembered none of it. The whole picture in front of her proceeded without a sound. Like a silent movie. The carriage had come to a screeching stop, the four horses stood snorting and stamping distractedly. She looked down to see her mother's body, which had been wrenched from her hand, lying like a mangled doll in the gutter. Eszter lay there like the twisted corn doll she carried with her all the time and which was now lying on the road next to her hand where it had been released at the moment she was trampled by the horses. Eva stepped forward and retrieved the doll from the dirt. As she did so, she could see that blood was seeping from her mother's head onto the road and that she was not moving, lying there absolutely still like a corn doll herself, with no sign of life. Over the last ten years Eva had carried with her a vague but horrific memory of when, as a toddler, her mother had fallen over a curb stone in the road by the house they lived in, unconscious and bleeding badly down her legs. Luckily, her mother had made a complete recovery from that accident. But this was different.

Eva knew at once that her mother was dead, but could not process the fact. She found herself sitting on the curb stone next to her mother's body, grazed and badly bruised herself. But that was of no import. Her mother's life and hopes and dreams had been erased – along with her own – in a second. At the very moment they had been celebrating together their escape from their tortured homeland and their new life in the future.

* * *

Eva remained on the pavement shaking and in tears. She watched as crowds of people thronged around her mother's dead body. Within a few minutes the police were on the scene, holding up the traffic and blowing their whistles, clearing the road around where her mother was lying. The driver of the carriage was standing by the roadside, shaking in distress and being interviewed by one of the policemen. Very quickly, a big square khaki ambulance with a huge red cross on its side had arrived. Her mother's body was lifted onto a stretcher and into the ambulance, driven off away from her before she could say goodbye. Eva continued to sit just where she was, on the hard curb stone, frozen by the horror and disbelief about what had just occurred. Within only a short space of time the gathering of onlookers and helpers started to disperse one by one to go on with their lives.

Nobody seemed to have noticed a twelve year old girl in tears on the pavement, at the place where her mother had died. Of if they did, nobody seemed to have guessed that this little girl might be the daughter of the dead woman herself. They must have all assumed that she was just one of the other passers-by, shocked by what she had just witnessed. Either way, the crowd thinned rapidly, chattering excitedly amongst themselves as they went about their business.

Eva could not stop the tears that continued to pour down her face. She held her small white handkerchief up to her eyes to quench the flow, but not because she wanted to stop the tears. She knew that this would not happen. She started to look around her. She realised that she was now alone, in all senses of the word. 'Why has this happened to me?' she couldn't help asking herself. She'd had friends who had lost one or both of their parents in the war, but she knew of no other child back home in Budapest who had lost their mother in such a tragic, pointless way. The old feeling she often had that she was 'somehow different' bubbled to the surface of her thoughts as she sat there on the curb side, but this time in a black, destructive way. She was sorry for her mother, who was now in another place, her life having been cut tragically short. But she couldn't stop feeling sorry for herself as well, and could not understand why life had dealt her this cruel blow.

* * *

After about half an hour Eva was still sitting where she had landed on the pavement. She did not have the will to get up, let alone to move on. She was alone in this city – this place to which she had arrived with her mother in the triumph of freedom – and had no idea what she should do next. She had no clue where she should go and was too frightened to approach any of the passing strangers to ask them for help.

At that moment a man and his wife who were passing stopped next to where she was sitting and bent down to speak to her. They could not have seen the terrible accident that had led to her mother's death, and it was likely therefore that they had no idea why Eva might have been sitting there crying. The pool of her mother's blood on the roadside had been quickly covered over with sawdust from a bucket hanging on the back of the carriage by a well-meaning person, before the horses and carriage had been led away from the scene..

'Are you alright, dear?' the woman asked her in German. 'Can we do anything to help?' her husband asked kindly, after Eva had not replied. The man and woman stood there awkwardly, not wanting to interfere, but not able to walk on and leave a child who was clearly in distress.

Eva's tear-stricken face looked up at the friendly, well-meaning couple. 'Can you help me, please? I've nowhere to go . . .'

CHAPTER 40

Eva woke the next morning to see a shaft of sunshine flooding into the room through a gap in the curtains. The minute dust particles in the air were dancing a sunshine dance, unaware of the grief she could still feel in her heart. Rosa and Jürgen Bruns – for that was their names – had taken her by the hand from where she was sitting on the pavement outside the main railway station and led her home to their nearby apartment in Liechtensteinstrasse, which was in a prosperous part of the city.

Rosa fed her supper that evening, and she and her husband listened quietly while Eva told them about the flight by train from Hungary she and her mother had made only the night before. Eva had not finished telling them the details, when Jürgen lifted the evening newspaper he had been reading before supper and pointed to its front page to Rosa behind Eva's back. They simultaneously realised with horror that Eva was the young daughter of the woman who had been trampled to death the previous afternoon by a horse drawn carriage right outside the Hauptbahnhof station. They had just been discussing the tragedy that had appeared on the newspaper's front page. Now they realised the reason why this young girl had been sitting on the side of the pavement weeping, and why it was she had not been able to tell them yet what her distress was all about.

* * *

A few days' later Rosa and Jürgen accompanied Eva to her mother's funeral. It was already the beginning of November, and the air was cold and damp as they walked into the cemetery hand in hand, one on either side of Eva. Jürgen had gone to the town hall to find out what had happened to Eszter's body. He had been told that an autopsy had already taken place and that the inquest into Eszter's death had concluded that the cause of death was accidental. A number of passers-by had come forward to the police to say that the accident was not the fault of the driver of the carriage. Eszter had stepped suddenly out in front of his carriage – dazzled by the low lying bright sunshine, perhaps – and he'd had no time to pull the horses up or take evasive action. Jürgen had arranged for Eszter's burial and paid for the internment.

They were the only people at the graveside, apart from the priest. As the coffin was lowered into the grave, Eva let go of Rosa's hand, walked forward a step and gently scattered some white lilies that Rosa had given her over her mother's coffin. The priest said a few words, a short time after which they turned and left, disappearing into the murky November evening, back into the city and the warmth of the Bruns' apartment.

The next morning the Bruns were up and sitting at the kitchen table when Eva woke up and walked in to join them. Rosa sat her down next to them and placed a bowl of hot porridge on the table in front of her.

'Tell us, Eva,' Rosa asked her, as Eva ate the porridge. What family do you have back in Budapest?'

'There is no-one,' Eva replied. 'Only my mother and I lived together. My father Robert was around when I was young – he was drunk most of the time – but he came and went until one day he went out at night and never came back. Before him there was my mother's friend Peter, who my mother told me she loved very much. But he left us after my father came back from the labour camp in the war. Mother told me Peter went back to his family in Poland. We never saw him again after that.'

'I see,' said Rosa. So you have no other family or relatives – grandparents or uncles and aunts elsewhere, perhaps?'

'No, they were all killed in the gas chambers.'

Rosa and Jürgen looked at each other. 'Would you like to stay with us then, to come and live with us here? We have no children of our own and we would like to look after you until you are old enough to lead your own life.'

'Thank you, Rosa,' Eva said. 'I would.'

CHAPTER 41

Eva settled in to her life with the Bruns with little difficulty. She knew at the age of twelve that she had no-one else to go to, nowhere else to live. She missed her mother and never ceased to grieve for her. They had only been together for what now seemed such a short time. But the Bruns were also kind and decent people and, as was the case with many orphaned children before her, with time she fell in love with her new parents and became happy in her new life with them. After she had been with them for two years, the Bruns adopted her formally as their own child.

Eva was a bright girl and did well at school. It did not take her long to be fluent in German as well as her native Hungarian, and she usually came near the top of the class in most subjects. She passed her matriculation with no problems.

* * *

Just before Eva reached her eighteenth birthday, Rosa and Jürgen sat down with her one evening.

'What would you like to do when you have finished school, Eva?' Jürgen asked her.

'I would like to train to be a nurse,' Eva replied without hesitation. She had been thinking about her future herself for some time and was already set on this idea.

'Where would you like to do this?' Rosa asked her.

'Nowhere in particular. Have you any suggestions?' Eva replied.

'As it happens,' Rosa said, 'I have a sister, Isabelle, who is a trained nurse in London. I had an idea that you might be interested in becoming a nurse and have already spoken to her on the telephone. She said she would be happy to have you to live with her while you are training, if that is what you want. What do you think about going to train as a nurse in London?'

'That would be exciting!' Eva replied.

* * *

Eva leant out of the train window to kiss Rosa and Jürgen goodbye one last time. She'd barely had time to catch her breath in excitement as phone calls and letters were exchanged between Vienna and London and her travel plans all put in place. Isabelle was looking forward to welcoming Eva to live with her in her house in Highbury, and had very kindly offered to put her up without any charge for board or lodging while she was training to be a nurse. Jürgen and Rosa had given her a very generous gift of money as her eighteenth birthday present – most of it already converted into British pounds. She had sewn the wad of unfamiliar notes into the inside lining of her overcoat for safe keeping. She had nothing to worry her, and could not have been more excited about the journey ahead.

She waved her final goodbye to her adoptive parents as the train started to pull away from the station. As it did so, the memory of the triumphant arrival she'd made with her mother to that very same station six years before came flowing back to her. They had both been so happy and excited about their future then, but the future for her mother Eszter had been extinguished in a flash. As the train picked up speed, carrying her away to a new life, Eva could not help but feel excited about her own future now, about the next move she was making in her life, in spite of the reminder of her mother's tragic death this train journey gave her. Yet again, her feeling of being 'somehow different' bubbled to the surface. Out of the tragedy of her mother's death had come an exciting opportunity that was being opened up to her in a way she could never have imagined. She took a moment to say a prayer to her mother and ask her to look over her in the next step on her journey.

* * *

The train from Vienna stopped at Munich, where she had to change, and then other trains took her on to Paris and then to Calais. When she arrived off the boat as a foot passenger at the port of Dover, Isabelle was there to meet her, wearing a red rose in the lapel of her jacket, as she had promised to do. Eva liked her immediately. She was Rosa's younger sister, equally as warm and friendly as Rosa and Jürgen, and happy to welcome Eva, whom she had never met before, as a young woman starting out in adult life. They took a train to London and, on arrival at Charing Cross station, a bus trip through the centre of the capital to Isabelle's house in Highbury.

Isabelle showed Eva to a spare room at the top of her modest but comfortable town house and left her to unpack. Eva spent the next hour or two making herself at home, unpacking her luggage, placing her clothes in the chest of drawers and her books and belongings along the shelves and in the bookcase. She was more excited than she had ever been about the new life ahead of her.

CHAPTER 42

1962

'Tell us, Miss Bruns, Miss Watling and I would like to know why you want to train as a nurse?'

'I believe it is a noble profession and that it would be a privilege to care for the sick and needy, Miss Wordsworth,' Eva replied without hesitation, looking both women straight in the eye, as she had been advised to do.

'Yes, yes,' Miss Wordsworth continued her interrogation, firing questions at her like a machine gun. 'But why should we offer a training place to you here at St Thomas's Hospital rather than any of the other candidates whom we are interviewing this morning? What credentials do you have that would persuade us to accept you onto our State Registered Nurse training course? Do you have any experience yet in caring for other people? Have you ever seen a dead body?'

'Only once that I remember,' Eva hesitated, somewhat surprised by the rather direct questioning, choosing to answer the last question first.

'Under what circumstances?' Miss Wordsworth persisted.

'In 1956, when I was twelve, I witnessed my own mother being trampled to death next to me by a horse drawn carriage in Vienna as we came out of the railway station. We had just arrived off the overnight train after escaping from our home in Hungary before the Soviet troops invaded. In 1944 I had also been surrounded by people who were dead and dying on the train to Auschwitz where I and my mother and her family were being transported to, but I was a baby then and only learnt about the horror of that journey from my mother when I was older.'

'I see,' said Miss Wordsworth, taken aback. 'You obviously have lived a very eventful life,' she pronounced in understatement. 'Now, let's look at your school report and examination grades.'

From then on the interview progressed in a much less formal way. The two nursing tutors became almost friendly towards her, clearly wanting to defuse any embarrassment their initial questioning may have caused the candidate. Eva relaxed and answered all their questions honestly.

'We have no more questions, Miss Bruns,' Miss Watling concluded the interview. 'We thank you for taking the trouble to apply to our prestigious Hospital. The interview is finished. You will be hearing from us by post within the next week.'

Eva shook both women politely by the hand and left the interview room. She had left her home in Vienna with the Bruns when she reached her eighteenth birthday and travelled to England on her own. As soon as she was settled with Rosa's sister Isabelle in London, she had enlisted in a night school in Camden Town where she did an intensive English course. She hadn't come all this way to be defeated now and was determined to succeed with her career. She returned to her digs with Isabelle from the interview at St Thomas's Hospital confident that she would be successful.

CHAPTER 43

Eva was perhaps as happy as she had ever been in her life, training to be a state registered nurse. The student nurses at St Thomas's Hospital were kept under a strict but fair regime. They had to be turned out neatly with fresh uniform, polished shoes and clean starched white aprons every day. Hardly a day went by when they were not reminded by one or other of their nursing tutors or ward sisters that they were being trained to step into the exalted footsteps of Florence Nightingale. Indeed, upon graduation they would become fully qualified 'Nightingales' – with all the prestige and honour that that title carried. Not to mention the regulation frilly lace hats which all Nightingales got to wear.

Rosa's sister Isabelle looked after Eva as if she was her own sister. She was not over-bearing, allowing Eva to be out and about in London whenever and wherever she pleased, and never questioned Eva about where she had gone the night before, and at what time she got back. At the same time she encouraged Eva as an older sister might have done, making sure she was punctual for shifts and lectures at all times and ensuring that she was taking her studying seriously, handing in all her essays and projects in time for the deadlines that had been set.

* * *

It was a Saturday evening, about six months after Eva had arrived to live with Isabelle in London. She had been out for the evening with some of the other trainee nurses who were in her introductory year at St Thomas's Hospital. Isabelle was still up, sitting in front of the fire reading the evening newspaper. Eva took off her coat and sat down with her, telling Isabelle excitedly about all of the new friends she had made.

'I remember what it was like,' Isabelle said, smiling at Eva's excitement.

'Did you train as a nurse here in London too?' Eva asked her 'aunt'. She realised that she had been too busy with her own affairs since arriving in England to ask Isabelle about how she had ended up living and working there in London.

'No, I trained as a nurse in Vienna before the war, but came to London very soon after qualifying. In 1938, I volunteered to help with the *Kindertransport*, accompanying a group of young children who were leaving by train from Vienna on their way to England. The evacuation had been arranged by an organisation which had been set up to rescue mostly Jewish children from German occupied Austria prior to the onset of the Second World War. I was only twenty one myself, and had never travelled outside Austria before, so it was a great venture for me too. I was part of the group led by a Dutch woman called Geertruida Wijsmuller-Meijer to bring the first transport of children out of Vienna.

'You cannot imagine how traumatic the parting was, both for the parents who were sending their children away – perhaps for ever – to unknown new homes in England, and for the children themselves. They had been told that they were going on an exciting journey, that it was only a short trip and that they would only be away a little while. There were many tears and even screaming. The very young children in particular could not understand why they were leaving their parents and demanded to stay with them. The children had to be gently lifted away from their mothers' arms and up onto the train. Each child was only allowed to take a small sealed suitcase with no valuables and no more than ten marks in money. Some were leaving with nothing but a cardboard tag on their front and their name on their back.

'Our train left Vienna on 10 December 1938 with 600 children. We came by boat from the Hook of Holland near Rotterdam to the port of Harwich, arriving from there by train at Liverpool Street Station in London. We were met at the station by all those kind people who had volunteered to look after the children as foster parents.

'After I arrived in London I felt very much at home here, in spite of the national anxieties of the impending war. When I had completed my responsibility to 'my' children, and had ensured that they had all been satisfactorily placed in caring homes, I made the decision to stay here myself. I was not happy about the idea of returning to Austria, which had been occupied by Germany and seemed to me to be collaborating in many ways with Hitler's Nazis. The plan to bring the Jewish children to Britain was launched not long after the devastation of Kristallnacht – the 'Night of Broken Glass', the pogrom against Jews in Germany, Austria and the Sudetenland carried out by SA paramilitary forces, following which shards of broken glass littered the streets after the windows of Jewish shops, buildings and synagogues were smashed. Many Jews were murdered and it was clear that this would not be an isolated incident in the persecution of Jewish people, as indeed turned out to be the case. Our escape with Jewish children from Austria occurred only a month after this horrible event. I did not have any doubts about staying here in England. I had no wish to go back to Nazi occupied Austria. I applied for a job as a trained nurse in the capital and have lived and worked here since. I have not been back to Austria since that day.'

Eva was amazed to hear Isabelle's story, which was in many ways as remarkable as hers had been. As she lay in bed that night thinking about what she had heard, she realised why it was that Isabelle had welcomed her so warmly to live with her when Rosa had put the idea to her.

Eva bought a second hand bicycle and took to riding it to work and all around London on her days off. Cycling down from Highbury to St Thomas' was a fair stretch, but she always left herself plenty of time, especially when on duty in the early morning and prior to a night shift in the evenings, when she had to deal with the rush hour traffic at its heaviest. After a few weeks of bike riding everywhere, she realised that her physical fitness – which was very good before – was becoming even better. She was also acutely aware, however, that bicycle riding in London carried a significant risk. If nothing else, she learnt this from a stint she'd had in the casualty department, where inevitably she witnessed many road casualties being brought in by ambulance, including quite a few fatalities. Sadly, a number of the latter were young women cyclists.

When she made this observation to one of the young male casualty officers, he replied that this is because the women were not as strong as the men. She thought initially that he was being a misogynist, until he went on to explain that many of those that died in cycle accidents did so as a result of being caught under the wheels of heavy goods vehicles, often as the lorry turned a corner without the driver being able to see the cyclist in the blind spot of his rear view mirror. He went on to explain that, when cyclists found themselves in a critical situation like this, it was often the young men who had the strength to pull themselves and their bike out of the way in a hurry, whilst the smaller young women sometimes did not have the strength to do so, and perished. Eva took even greater care going home in the dusk that evening.

In spite of the long hours and heavy duties, the social life was great. She soon found her way around London, made easier on a bike than it would have been travelling underground on a tube train to and from work every day. She got to know where the theatres, cinemas and concerts halls were situated, and was happy to find that the choice of music concerts was as wide as it was in Vienna, if not more so. She was popular among her nursing colleagues, who were generally quite a bit younger than she was and tended to look up to her for ideas and advice. She was also a pretty young woman in her mid-twenties by now, and although not taken to flaunt the fact, secretly enjoyed the admiration this brought her from women and men alike. She was never short of a girl or boy friend to go to a concert or film with, and she was always invited to the nurses' dos and the junior doctors mess parties.

Eva had a succession of adoring, nice boyfriends during this time. But she always made it clear to them at the outset that her main focus in life was to pass her nurse registration – with flying colours if possible – and that she would not let an overindulgent social life ruin this ambition.

CHAPTER 44

January, 1964

P eter awoke with a start. Someone was hammering loudly and repeatedly on the front door of the farmhouse. He looked at the clock. It was 4 a.m. and still dark outside.

'I'm coming,' he called to whoever the intruders were. Julia was starting to stir in the bed beside him. 'It must be something serious,' he said to himself as he jumped out of bed, throwing on his dressing gown as he ran to the door. Perhaps there was a fire in the barn? Please God, not that. He screwed back the rusty bolts and threw the door open.

Two men were standing right in front of him. They were wearing unfamiliar police uniforms and spoke to him in German.

'Peter Leahy?' one demanded. 'Yes,' he replied.

'We are arresting you under the State laws of the Federal Republic of Germany. You do not have to say anything at this stage. We are taking you into custody pending your trial in front of the Second Auschwitz Court.' They swivelled him round and cuffed his hands behind his back. Peter said nothing. He didn't resist.

Julia appeared behind him at that moment, clutching her dressing gown cord tight around her. 'Darling, what's going on!' she cried.

'I'm not sure, but I think I can guess,' was all he could say to his wife.

'Where are you taking him?' she shouted to the men who were now marching her husband down the path towards the open back doors of a police van.

'To Frankfurt am Main in Germany,' they shouted back, as they bundled Peter into the back of the van, jumped into the front themselves and drove off.

He had not even had time to say goodbye to Julia.

* * *

Peter sat in the back of the van as it sped along motorways on its way to Germany and Frankfurt. He was not completely surprised by this sudden intrusion into his simple domestic life in Poland. Ever since the end of the war he had known that it was possible that he might be apprehended for his role as an SS guard at Birkenau, however accidental and innocent his presence there had been on his part. But he was surprised that it had taken twenty years for them to catch up with him. He had read about the public international trials of the prominent Nazi leaders at the War Crimes Tribunal in Nuremberg in 1945-46 and the subsequent Auschwitz trial in November and December 1947. The latter had taken place in Krakow, not far from where he still lived. The Polish Supreme National Tribunal had tried forty former staff of the Auschwitz concentration camps and many had been sentenced to death by hanging. Although this was front page news in all the Polish newspapers at the time, Peter had never discussed with Julia the possibility that he too might be apprehended as well at some time in the future. He found it better to live in hope and, however it might seem from the outside, he had a clear conscience about the enforced role which had been thrust upon him during the two months he had been a guard at the Birkenau railhead.

Following these trials, and after so many years had passed, he had thought he might now be free from arrest. But after the twists and turns his life had taken, nothing really surprised him anymore. He knew he had to face his fate once more.

CHAPTER 45

Peter had been sitting handcuffed for hours in this poorly lit dank basement corridor with a long line of other prisoners who were waiting for their cases to be heard that day. The other prisoners were grumbling to themselves or to the prisoner sitting next to them. One man opposite him seemed to be staring constantly in his direction, as if he wanted to catch his eye, to make contact; but Peter ignored him and everyone else around him, not feeling like getting into a conversation with anyone. The time seemed to pass slowly, but he supposed this was something to do with how the passage of justice was measured.

He was finally pulled to his feet by two guards and marched along the basement corridor. He was ready for whatever his fate might be and walked with his head held high, his hands cuffed in front of him. He knew in his heart that he was innocent of any charges they might wish to bring against him. They came to the end of the corridor and the guards pushed him up some steep steps into the bright light of the courtroom. He stood there, blinking in the bright lights, needing to adapt to the surroundings he had been thrust up into. The dock he found himself in was barred all round and encased in glass. He had been in custody for weeks and now the time had finally come to face his accusers.

The Bürgerhaus Gallus in Frankfurt am Main had been converted to hear the Second Auschwitz Trials, the court cases that were taking place under German criminal law to try all those other mid- to lower-level officials in the Auschwitz-Birkenau death and concentration camp complex who were now at last being indicted for their roles in the Holocaust. Looking around, he could see that it was a large courtroom, packed with people. There were scores of international observers and journalists, as well as crowds of people in the public gallery at the back of the court behind him. A number of microphones hung from the ceiling, like large black predatory spiders, waiting to record the proceedings, and the court officials and lawyers had ear pieces in their ears to receive translation when this was necessary.

'All stand!' the clerk of the court barked out in German, and the whole court rose to its feet as the three judges entered from the rear of the court. The judges mounted the raised dais at the front of the court, dressed in black gowns with purple satin sashes running diagonally from one shoulder to the opposite hip. They bowed solemnly to the assembly and sat down at the bench in the front of the court. The table at which they sat was covered in a gold cloth. On the wall behind them was hung a placard with the title of the court:

Der Zweite Auschwitz-Prozess/The Second Auschwitz Trials

The senior judge was sitting in the centre of his two colleagues, his name on a label on the table in front of him: Hans Hofmeyer, Chief Judge. He opened the hearing. 'This is the continued hearing of the Second Auschwitz Trials being held under the State Laws of the Federal Republic of Germany. The court is now in session. The next case number 142 is that of former Birkenau SS guard Peter Leahy.'

Judge Hofmeyer addressed him directly: 'Peter Leahy, you are brought in front of the Second Auschwitz Trials today accused of murder. Namely that, between May 1944 and July 1944 you, as a member of the Schutzstaffel guarding the death camp at Auschwitz-Birkenau, were responsible for inhumane practices against innocent prisoners leading to their murder by gas.'

'I invite the lead prosecutor to open the case.'

The State Attorney General Fritz Bauer rose to his feet, his hands gripping the top of his gown, and also turned to address his opening statement to Peter directly. 'Peter Leahy, you are charged with murder and other crimes committed under your own initiative between May and July 1944 at the Birkenau concentration camp. We have documents from the camp records confirming that you were an SS camp guard during that time and will if necessary call into the court witnesses who are prepared to confirm your identity and collusion in these crimes.' The chief prosecutor jerked his black robe tight across his shoulders with his hands and sat down again after this brief introductory statement, pouring himself a glass of water from the decanter on his desk as he did so.

Peter understood what the chief prosecutor meant when he said that he was being prosecuted for crimes which he had committed under 'his own initiative'. He had read from the details of the previous trials that the court did not consider that it was an acceptable defence for an accused to claim that they were acting under orders from their superior officers: an 'ordinary soldier doing his duty', even though this had been true in his case, as far as he was concerned. He was being tried as an individual perpetrator of these crimes in which role he was considered to be just as guilty as those above him.

Peter's lawyer Walter Blöck sat on the legal benches to the right of the defendants' box in which he was standing. He had looked up to acknowledge Peter as he entered the box from below. He was a young graduate lawyer, quite a bit younger than Peter himself. Peter had only had one opportunity to discuss his trial with him the previous afternoon, and then only for a short time. They had agreed that there was no point in Peter denying that he had acted as a guard at the railhead to Birkenau concentration camp for a brief period in 1944. Peter made clear to the lawyer, however, that he intended to plead not guilty to the crimes he was being accused of. Blöck was not so sure that this was such a good idea, and tried to persuade Peter that he might hope for a more lenient sentence if he were to plead guilty. But Peter was adamant that he had done nothing wrong or inhumane and that he required Blöck to defend him robustly against the charges.

'In which case, is there nobody you could call upon to speak in your defence?' the lawyer had asked him at that brief meeting. 'Perhaps a member of your battalion, for example, who could vouch for the fact that you were not engaged in inhumane practices during the time you were a guard at the Birkenau railhead?'

Peter sat and thought for a few minutes. 'I had no colleagues that I was close to – let alone friendly with – during the short time I was serving with the SS camp guard platoon. It wasn't like that. From my point of view it was such a grim situation for me to find myself in, a position that I found out was abhorrent but was unable to get out of. This wasn't the case with my fellow guards, as far as I could see. Most if not all of them appeared to have no such reservations about their participating in the killings. In fact most of them seemed to relish their part in murdering these innocent people. That was the main reason why I did not develop any friendships with my fellow guards. I've certainly had no contact with any of my platoon since, for the same reason.' Blöck sat there making notes.

Peter sat thinking for a few minutes more, before continuing.

'You are probably not aware that I was arrested myself and dismissed from my posting as an SS camp guard at Birkenau in July 1944 after I had allowed a young girl and her baby to escape at the railhead? When I was hauled up in front of my platoon commander I assumed I was going to be found guilty, taken out and shot. But instead he dismissed me from the SS and demoted me back into the ranks of a private soldier in the Wehrmacht. Following this, I was imprisoned in the camp cells and left for months in solitary confinement. Surely all that should also be on my records, if they have access to them? When I was eventually removed from the prison, I was fortunate enough to escape while being transported out of the camp to another destination. I am not sure whether the guards were ever aware of my escape. They certainly never came after me. That probably won't be on my records!' he said with a wry smile.

'After I escaped from detention myself, I went to Budapest to search for the girl. I found her there and lived with her for a short time, but I had to leave when her husband re-appeared. After that, I came back to live with my parents on their farm in Southern Poland, where I have lived since. I've had no contact with the girl, Eszter, since that time and have no idea where she might be living now or how I might find her while under arrest here. I feel very fatalistic about the outcome of this trial, he added.

'The information you have given me about the fact that you yourself were arrested for allowing a prisoner to escape is potentially very helpful,' Blöck agreed with him, 'but only if you were to have someone who could give evidence in your defence that this story is true. Without such evidence, I fear, it does not sound good,' his lawyer said, shuffling his papers in embarrassment. Peter stared at the lawyer: he couldn't be sure that even the man defending him believed his story.

Blöck had concluded their meeting by warning Peter that he feared that, in this situation, there was little he would be able to do to mitigate the accusations against him which were in front of the court. He was explicit in telling his client that, under the circumstances, he should expect to be found guilty and given a life sentence or maybe even sentenced to death, depending on how the court chose to deal with others of a similar rank who had been involved in the running of the concentration camps.

Peter now stood in the defendants' box, his legs shaking under him, recalling his lawyer's conclusions the previous day.

'Many times man lives and dies . . .' the quote from his favourite Irish poet came back into his mind once more, just as it had when he'd been arrested on the first occasion in Birkenau. Only this time his mind was not as clear as it had been when he'd been arraigned in front of his commanding officer, accused of allowing his beloved Eszter and her baby to escape from his guard at the railhead of the concentration camp. This time he felt sure luck would not be on his side. This time he felt that it was unlikely that he could persuade the court that there were any mitigating factors which would tip the scales in his favour. He couldn't deny the fact that he had been a member of the Birkenau SS guard for a short time, and they would naturally decide that his behaviour in that role had been as tainted as all the other guards. He felt fatalistic. He had no idea who they might bring before the court to identify him as having been one of the SS guards, but in any case they had apparently found the camp records with his name on it. He had already started to accept the likelihood that he would receive a guilty verdict.

The Chief Judge Hans Hofmeyer sat forward addressing Peter again.

'Please confirm to the court that you are Peter Leahy, a German citizen.'

'I am Peter Leahy,' Peter replied to the judge in a quiet but clear voice. 'But I am a Polish citizen. I was born and brought up by my Polish parents in Brzezinka, a small village in southern Poland.'

'I see,' said the judge staring incredulously over his half-moon spectacles. 'Then how was it as a Polish citizen that you became a member of the SS guard at the Auschwitz-Birkenau concentration camp? We have your name and details from the camp records in front of us. You do not deny that you were involved in that capacity?' Peter sensed that the judge thought he was lying, in an attempt to save his skin.

'When the Germans invaded Poland I was captured with my two brothers and the other young men of our battalion of the Polish army who were guarding the border. We were being lined up to be shot. I and my brothers explained to our captors that we were, in fact, German citizens. This was not a lie, since my father had been born in Germany and we therefore held duel German and Polish citizenship. We were lucky enough to have our identity cards showing our German citizenship by virtue of our father's birth with us. These were accepted as genuine by the German army officer in charge, and all three of us were released from detention. We were, however, immediately enlisted into the German army, the Wehrmacht, without the chance for dissent. I don't know what happened to my brothers after that. I served in the Wehrmacht for over four years, during which I was transferred through a number of different postings.'

'I see,' the judge said, looking sideways at his two colleagues, clearly thinking this was a ruse on Peter's behalf to avoid a guilty sentence. 'But somehow you next became a member of the Auschwitz SS guard, which to my knowledge would have been unheard of for a man who was also Polish. You do not deny that?'

'No, Sir,' Peter replied. 'I do not deny this. In May 1944 I was transferred to Birkenau as an ordinary SS guard. I did not apply for this posting. I had not admitted the fact that I had Polish as well as German citizenship when I was enlisted into the Wehrmacht. But during my two months at the camp I was only ever on guard duty at the railhead to Birkenau, guarding the prisoners as they arrived off the trains. I was never involved with their horrific murders which I very soon learned were taking place within the camp itself. I never carried out a single violent act towards any of the prisoners.'

All this was the truth, but Peter could sense that the judge was patently unimpressed by his evidence. 'He has heard it all before,' Peter thought to himself. Almost every man and woman who came before the tribunal very likely tried to concoct some sort of mitigating evidence to save their skins, he supposed. The judge was clearly bored by it all.

'Do you plead guilty or not guilty to the crimes with which you are charged?' Judge Hofmeyer put to him.

'Not guilty, Sir,' Peter replied without hesitation.

'At this juncture,' the judge said, looking at his watch, 'I call a recess. We will re-convene and continue with this defendant in one hour.'

* * *

CHAPTER 46

The court re-convened after the judges had had an hour's break for their lunch. Peter had been given a glass of warm water. He stood up back in the defendants' box feeling faint in the heat of the bright lights bearing down on him.

'We resume the hearing with the evidence in the case of Peter Leahy, case number 142,' the senior judge announced to the re-assembled court. 'The defendant has pleaded 'Not guilty' to the charges in front of him, but at the same time has admitted to being an SS camp guard at Birkenau in 1944. At this point, the court' – indicating to his fellow judges either side of him – 'would like if possible to avoid the witnesses for the prosecution going through the trauma of re-living their memories of their time incarcerated in Birkenau. It would therefore be helpful at this juncture to know the views of the counsel for the defence on this matter.

'Do you wish to present any evidence in defence of the accused, and if so does this include calling any witnesses of your own?' the judge asked Peter's lawyer, looking towards him on the lawyer's desk.

At that moment Peter saw his young lawyer Walter Blöck leaning sideways towards a clerk who had tapped him on the shoulder, presented him with a note and stood whispering in his ear. The lawyer nodded in understanding and sprang to his feet.

'Yes Sir. We do have a witness who wishes to speak in defence of Peter Leahy.'

'In that case, the court would like to hear what he or she has to say before calling the witnesses that the Chief Prosecutor has in hand, to spare them unnecessary distress if possible. This is the sequence that the court has already adopted when hearing the cases of previous accused, for the same reason,' the Chief Judge added, as a clarification for any persons who had just joined the court proceedings.

'Very good, Sir,' Peter's lawyer jumped at the offer which had been made. 'I call as witness for the defence Herr Ralph Schön.' The judge raised an eyebrow in surprise and there was a brief shuffle in the court. A man in handcuffs was brought up from below the court in to the witness box to the left of the defendants' box where Peter was standing. Peter gasped with disbelief as he recognised the man. It was the prisoner who had been staring across the corridor at him as they sat in the line waiting for their cases to be called. For the first time Peter remembered where he had met the man before.

'You are Ralph Schön?' Peter's lawyer stood to question the witness. 'And you have been a defendant in this war crimes trial yourself?'

'Yes Sir, that is correct,' Schön replied in an educated German accent.

'What is the basis of your indictment?' His lawyer's questioning continued.

'That I was a Hauptmann platoon commander of SS guards at Birkenau from May 1944 to January 1945. That I am charged with having been responsible for the murder of prisoners in that role.'

'And why are you appearing in front of this court as a witness in the defence of the accused, Peter Leahy?'

'Because I recognised him in the cell, have been told what he has said in his defence and can confirm that it is true.'

'Please go on,' Peter's lawyer encouraged him.

'Firstly,' the man began, 'it is true that Leahy was an SS guard in my platoon. But in this capacity he was only ever a soldier responsible for guarding the prisoners from escaping as they arrived off the trains at the railhead to Birkenau. He was not involved in the selection of prisoners for the gas chambers. And he had no other duties within the camp itself.

'Secondly, and most importantly in his case, in July 1944 he was himself arrested for allowing a young woman to escape with her baby as they descended from the wagon at the railhead to Birkenau. He was put on trial for this transgression and brought before me as his commanding officer for sentencing. I decided to show leniency, not to impose the death sentence on him, but dismissed him from the SS and returned him to the Wehrmacht. He was put into solitary confinement in the camp prison while waiting to be transferred out to his fate in the Wehrmacht.'

There was a pause while Peter's defending counsel took all this in. When he had done so, Walter Blöck addressed Schön again.

'How can the court be sure that you are not one prisoner coming to the aid of another, in an attempt to gain leniency for your colleague?' Peter's lawyer asked the man directly.

'I suppose they can't be sure with certainty.' Schön admitted with frankness. 'Except that I have already pleaded guilty to the charges brought against myself and have made my peace with my own God. I know that, if necessary, I deserve to die for my role in the camp, if that is the sentence that the court gives me. This man is innocent and does not deserve to die. I have not seen him or spoken to him since he was standing before me accused of helping a prisoner to escape and thereby avoid the death of herself and her baby in the gas chambers. As a result of that female prisoner's escape I myself was reprimanded, dismissed as platoon commander and imprisoned. I was only released from the camp prison when the Soviets liberated Birkenau in January 1945. I therefore have nothing to gain in speaking up in Leahy's defence now.'

As Schön finished speaking there was minor uproar in the court. The assembled knew they had been hearing something special.

'Quiet, please,' the senior judge commanded. He looked sideways and mouthed to the other two judges and they nodded in agreement. 'My colleagues and I will have a brief recession. Please stay seated.'

***

CHAPTER 47

After less than five minutes, the three judges reappeared on the podium.

'Court, please stand,' the clerk instructed. During this further recess Peter remained standing where he was in the defendant's box.

'Peter Leahy,' the senior judge began, looking straight at Peter. 'The court accepts the evidence which you have given, and that of the prisoner who has spoken in your defence. We have based our decision on the precedent set by the First Auschwitz Trial in the case of Sergeant Major Hans Münch, who was found to have refused to participate in the selection process of prisoners for the gas chambers and was therefore acquitted. The case is dismissed. You are free to go.'

Peter sat down immediately in surprise. He was helped up by one of the court guards, his handcuffs removed, and led away back down to the basement and out of the court.

***

Peter was stunned by the abrupt turn of events and the dismissal of the case against him. The pessimism about the certainty of his conviction which had enveloped him evaporated instantly. He left the court shaking and with an immense sense of relief.

He wasn't given the opportunity to speak to Ralph Schön and to thank him for being prepared to speak in his defence. He didn't know what he had done to deserve this support from the man, but his view of his former commanding officer changed completely as a result. Whatever the details of Schön's role in the mass murders which occurred at Birkenau, he hoped that the courage the man had shown in standing up for him might also be seen by the court as a mitigating factor in whatever sentence they were to give him.

There was no question of any reparation towards him, but Peter did not expect that. He was released by the back door of the court on to the street with no ceremony, but was given the money to buy himself a train ticket to return to

Krakow. He was a free man again, and had been given an official court letter attesting to the fact that he had been found innocent of all the charges against him. Within two days he was back with Julia. She was overjoyed that he had returned safely and thrilled to hear that the charges against him had finally been dropped.

Peter was pleased to be back home, but could not forget that, when he was first arrested, he had felt a strong need to let Eszter know what was happening. He knew she would have given evidence to the court in his defence if he had been able to contact her before facing trial. Now that he was a free man, he also wished he could have the opportunity to tell her the good news. He still could not get her out of his life and thoughts completely, especially at times of stress such as that he had just been through.

* * *

Three weeks after his release from arrest Peter was sitting in front of the wood fire at home after supper. He picked up the local paper he had brought back with him from the market at Rajko that afternoon. Tired from his day's work, he started to turn the pages without much enthusiasm. Suddenly the headline at the top of page three stared back at him: 'Auschwitz guilty sentences carried out'. The newspaper stated bluntly that sentences had been carried out the previous morning on those accused found guilty and condemned to death by the Second Auschwitz Trials which had been held in Frankfurt. The names of those who had been hanged for crimes against humanity were listed below.

Peter scoured the long list of condemned below the article. Towards the end of the list he came across the one name he had feared would be there:

'Ralph Schön, SS Hauptmann Camp Platoon Commander, Birkenau, aged 53 years.' Against his name there was a brief note stating that the accused had been found imprisoned in the guardhouse himself when Auschwitz was liberated, but that numbers of other prisoners freed from the camp at the same time had identified him as having been a camp platoon commander of Birkenau. Schön had been put to death by hanging at 07.00 h the previous morning.

Peter dropped the paper on his lap and sat there staring into space.

The man had been arrested and imprisoned by his superiors because of Peter's action in letting Eszter and her baby escape at the railhead. But the record that he had been a camp commander at Birkenau had eventually resulted in him facing the same court that Peter had himself and had led to his sentence to death.   Whatever the details of the man's crimes had been – and Peter realised they were likely to have been horrific – he had shown leniency to himself in not condemning him to death by firing squad, while knowing what his own fate was likely to be. Justice was never a singular event, Peter decided.

CHAPTER 48

1968

Eva loved night duty on the coronary care unit. As darkness fell and the lights were dimmed to allow the patients to sleep, she sat at the nursing desk with a dimmed angle poise lamp lowered above her paperwork, providing just enough light to allow her to write up her notes without disturbing the six men in the beds in front of her. The scene gave her a warm sense of homeliness and tranquillity, although she was alert enough to know that the latter could be shattered at any moment by a trolley clattering through the doors, bringing another very ill patient with it, or – worse still – one of the present crew going into cardiac arrest.

She was on her own in charge that night, but felt confident that she was now able to cope with the situation. The new Sister in charge of the CCU, Mary McFarlane, a Scottish woman, was an excellent nurse and had rejuvenated the CCU nursing team since she had taken over about four months before. Eva respected her a lot and had also grown very friendly with her. She was proud that Mary had become confident enough in her abilities that she had now given Eva the responsibility of being in charge alone on night duty, even though she was still a relatively junior staff nurse, only two years since she had qualified as a State Registered Nurse.

Eva looked at her watch. It was 3 a.m. already, and the six men on the unit all seemed to have finally settled to sleep at last, one or two of them snoring quite loudly. Eva looked at the console of monitors in front of her. The six cardiac traces showed that all of the patients were stable. Two of the patients had irregular heart beats, both having been in controlled atrial fibrillation for over twenty four hours now, the other four patients being in regular sinus rhythm. Eva looked down at the file which she was updating and continued writing up her notes. She was always very diligent about keeping up to date and relevant nursing notes, and Mary had complimented her about this on more than one occasion.

Suddenly the flashing light above her alerted her to the fact that the man in bed five had developed an abnormal heart rhythm. The monitor showed that his heart trace had become unstable and was throwing off multiple ventricular ectopics. Eva knew exactly what to do. She walked to his bedside and gently held his hand, which was warm. 'Are you OK, Ian?' she asked quietly. The man turned slightly towards her, still half asleep, and mumbled 'Yes thanks, nurse.' She could see that he was completely unaware of the change in his heart rhythm which had occurred, and that it was not giving him any pain or distress. She checked his blood pressure, which was normal. She knew, however, that he needed to be treated quickly because of the risk of him developing more serious complications such as ventricular fibrillation leading to heart failure and cardiac arrest.

Eva picked up the phone and asked the lady on switch to put an urgent call through to the on-call medical registrar. She knew from having talked to him on the phone earlier that Geoff had not left casualty all night, where he was dealing with dozens of medical emergency admissions. But she knew that this was urgent. If she didn't do something quickly the patient may very well go into cardiac arrest anyway. She got the arrest trolley ready next to the patient's bed. She checked in all the draws to make sure that everything she might need in the event of the patient arresting was in place and was pleased to find that it was. One of the ampoules her eye lingered over was the drug lignocaine. She knew at once that this was just the drug that the patient needed urgently to suppress his abnormal heart rhythm if his heart was to be prevented going into cardiac arrest. The phone on the desk rang.

'Hello. Geoff here. Got a problem, Eva?'

'Oh Geoff, very sorry to bother you. I know how busy you are. But the patient in bed five is throwing off frequent multi-focal ventricular ectopics. I think he needs intravenous lignocaine urgently to suppress them before her arrests.

'You're right, Eva,' Geoff replied. 'But I can't come up to you immediately.' He paused. 'Are you OK about accepting a verbal drug order? I'll come and write it up as soon as I can. We've got two patients undergoing cardiac resuscitation down here, as well as a whole bundle of acute medical emergency admissions.'

'Of course, Geoff. I understand. I'm happy to go ahead.' He gave her verbal instructions for setting up an intravenous lignocaine infusion on her patient.

She hung up a small bag of saline solution, drew up the liquid drug lignocaine and injected it in to the bag of saline. She then connected the bag of lignocaine solution to the cannula in the back of the patient's hand with a plastic giving set and opened the plastic tap on the giving set to start the drip running.

At that moment one of the orderlies put his head through the door: 'cup of tea, staff nurse?'

'Thanks very much, Brian,' Eva replied. 'Put it on the desk please.'

The orderly put the cup on the nurses' desk and went out. Eva went back to the desk to continue writing her notes and drink her cup of tea, leaving the drip going, knowing that she should let it run for about an hour initially. Over the next few minutes as she continued to keep a careful eye on bed five's ECG trace on the screen above her, she noticed with satisfaction from the monitor that the ectopic heart beats were starting to settle, becoming less and less frequent until they disappeared completely.

Eva was interrupted with a sudden start. The man in bed five was fitting violently, his arms and legs shaking uncontrollably; he was unconscious and grunting, foaming at the mouth. She rushed to his bedside, rolled him on to his left side, placed a plastic airway in his mouth and pulled up the bedside bars to make sure that he did not crash on to the floor as he fitted. She then placed an oxygen mask over his face. He was sweating profusely. Examining the drip, she realised with dismay that during the orderly's interruption with tea she had inadvertently left the giving set tap fully open. The bag had already nearly completely run through, giving him a much higher dose of lignocaine than she had intended, in a short space of time. Eva understood with horror that he was fitting as a result of her error. She knew she had no time to lose.

She shut off the drip and rushed to the drug cupboard, unlocked it and grabbed a vial of diazepam. Drawing this up with a needle and syringe as she hurried back to the patient's bed, she opened the plastic cap on the cannula in the back of the man's hand and started to inject the diazepam slowly into his vein. Very slowly, the fitting started to settle and eventually ceased completely.

The man's skin was sweating but became warm and well perfused again as his heart rhythm remained in regular sinus rhythm. He started to wake up. Eva removed the airway from his mouth and raised the head end of the bed, making him comfortable again on his back as she sat him up and re-arranged the pillows behind his head.

'It's all right, Ian,' she whispered into the man's ear. He turned and looked at her gratefully.

'Thanks a lot Eva,' he said. 'Could I have a cup of tea please?'

'In a little while,' she replied, stroking the sweat from his forehead with a cloth.

Once Ian was completely settled and she was confident that he remained in stable regular heart rhythm with no further sign of fitting, Eva returned to sit at her desk. For the first time she had the chance to consider the potential seriousness of the drug error she had just made. She knew the fact that she had administered the drug herself as an emergency, let alone the fact that she'd had nobody with her to check the dose of lignocaine she had given him, would be unlikely to mitigate how her actions would be judged. She would be in very serious trouble when it came to light, in spite of the fact that she had administered the correct antidote which had rapidly corrected the situation and had left the patient apparently unharmed.

Although she had administered the diazepam rapidly and correctly to abolish the man's fits, it had not been previously prescribed by a doctor. She knew that, if she were to admit what had happened to the Ward Sister when she came on duty at seven o'clock, Mary would have no choice but to report the incident. It would be recorded as a serious drug error. She also knew that she might well be suspended from duty pending an enquiry, and perhaps as a result even be struck-off by the General Nursing Council and lose her registration to practise. If this were to happen, all the years she had given up to train and become proficient in her nursing profession would have been wasted.

She walked over to the drug cupboard and stood there for some minutes grasping the drug cupboard shelf with both hands, anguishing about the situation. She was not prepared to contemplate the possibility that she might lose her fitness to practise as a result of this incident and be forced to give up the profession that she had trained so long for. With a heavy heart, she picked up the diazepam vial and the piece of glass she had broken off the top of it when opening it, and discarded them in the sharp's box. She sat down again at the nurses' desk feeling shattered by what had happened.

Mary and Heather, one of Eva's other staff nurse colleagues, came on duty at seven o'clock and they sat at the desk to hear Eva's report on the night shift she had just taken. When it came to Ian in bed five, Eva reported truthfully that, following his admission with a coronary thrombosis the day before, his heart had developed multiple ventricular ectopics in the early hours of that morning. She had contacted the medical registrar urgently about the need for a lignocaine infusion to suppress the ectopics and Geoff had agreed immediately. The problem had settled completely with the intravenous lignocaine drip which she had administered, and he had had no more ectopic activity since. All this was true, of course. She hadn't lied, but had omitted to mention the episode of fitting he had developed as a result of the inadvertent overdose of lignocaine he had received, as well as the correct but unauthorised treatment she had given him to rectify the fitting.

'Good girl,' Mary said, looking Eva straight in the eye, and pointedly without questioning her whether a doctor had been present at the time to supervise her decision. Geoff had called in at 6 a.m. when all was well, and had written up the lignocaine infusion retrospectively. Eva didn't mention this fact. She stared back at the Sister, her own eyes wary with lack of sleep, and said nothing more in reply.

Once she was back in her room in the nurses' home, Eva burst into tears, overwhelmed by exhaustion and the enormity of what she had done. She went over the events of the night before in her mind repeatedly. She knew she could not discuss this with anyone. But she knew in her heart that she had made the right decision not to mention her error, potentially serious though it had been, and that she would never make the same mistake again. She pulled the curtains shut and got in to bed knowing that she was unlikely to get much sleep before she was due back on duty later that night.

When she did return to work at eight o'clock the next night, nobody mentioned the fact that Ian had bitten his tongue, even if they had noticed it. Eva had cleaned the blood from his mouth and replaced the bloodied pillow case for a clean one, as she'd settled him down again following the seizures he had developed, and had given him a cube of ice to hold against his bitten tongue. When her hand-over report came to Ian in bed five, she asked as casually as she could about how he had been all that day. She was very relieved to hear that he was recovering well following his heart attack and was on course to be moved back to the general cardiac ward later the next day.

CHAPTER 49

1971

After three years working as a staff nurse, Eva decided she wanted to take more responsibility for her patients. In fact, she made up her mind that she wanted to become a doctor. She was pretty sure that her top marks she had obtained in science subjects at school in Vienna should be enough to get her into medical school; if she was a man, that was. She had come across one or two women doctors during her time at St Thomas's, but they were very much in a minority and she had a sense that there was still a great deal of difficulty for women to be accepted into what was traditionally a male dominated profession. She started to investigate where would be the best place for herself, as a female and 'mature' student, to apply to. After work one evening, she sat late in the library researching the places open to her to apply to. Her investigations led her to the Royal Free Hospital in Hampstead.

Eva read that the Royal Free Hospital had been founded in 1828 by the surgeon William Marsden to provide, as its name indicates, free care to those of little means. Eva was transfixed by his moving story. One night after dark, Marsden had found a young girl lying on the steps of St. Andrew Church, Holborn, dying from disease and hunger. He urgently sought help for her from some of the nearby hospitals. However, none would take the girl in and she died two days later. After this experience Marsden set up a small dispensary in Greville Street, Holborn, called the London General Institution for the Gratuitous Care of Malignant Diseases. A few years later, in 1832, a cholera epidemic – "King Cholera", as it had become named – arrived in England from Europe, killing about 6,500 people in London alone. At that time, the disease was thought to be spread by a "miasma" or bad smell in the atmosphere, a theory supported by leading figures in public health, including Florence Nightingale herself. Marsden's hospital extended care to many of the victims of the epidemic. The London Free Hospital, as it was now called, had been the only London hospital to treat victims of the cholera epidemic, as other voluntary hospitals in London refused to admit patients with infectious diseases. Five years later, in 1837, a royal charter was granted by the new young Queen Victoria to the hospital in recognition of its courageous act. From then on it was known as the Royal Free Hospital.

In the 1870s the Royal Free became a teaching hospital. For many years, the Royal Free Hospital had been the only London hospital allowing women who wanted to study medicine inside its walls. It formed an association with the London School of Medicine for Women, under which women from the school completed their clinical training at the hospital. The Royal Free medical school was established in 1877 under the Deanship of Elizabeth Garrett Anderson, one of the school's founders, and became part of the University of London in 1896, becoming known as the London Royal Free Hospital School of Medicine for Women.

As Eva read about the history of the Royal Free Hospital with enthusiasm, its reputation for admitting pioneering women graduates excited her and she knew that that was where she wanted to train as a doctor. She applied for entry and, to her joy, her application was successful. By the late 1960s the old site of the Hospital on Gray's Inn Road had become too cramped. A modern 12-storey cruciform tower block was built to replace it on the site of the former Hampstead Fever Hospital in Pond Street in Hampstead in the mid-1970s; it was opened by the Queen in 1978. Eva was proud to be one of the first year of clinical students to be admitted to the new hospital.

CHAPTER 50

Before starting on the wards, Eva had to spend three years studying her 'pre-clinical' subjects, which included anatomy, physiology, biochemistry and pharmacology. In the first week of this part of her training, she, along with all the other men and women in her year – there were seventy-five of them – made her first visit to the anatomy dissecting rooms, in the hospital basement. Gowned up with green surgical gowns, masks and rubber gloves they entered the large dissecting hall with a certain amount of trepidation. They had heard all the stories about this part of their training that was to come: rumours of students fainting on the floor or rushing out to the lavatories for fresh air. Eva was determined not to be one of these faint-hearted students, but she had to admit on her first visit that the over-powering smell of formalin – that colourless solution of formaldehyde in water used to preserve the bodies of the deceased persons who had donated their bodies after their deaths for the 'advancement of medical science' – was overwhelming. The solution may have been colourless – and apparently innocuous on inspection – but was certainly not innocuous to the smell. The pungent reek of the chemical formaldehyde caused a burning sensation in her nose and throat, and the waves of the fumes which hit her as she entered the dissecting room caused her eyes to smart and made it difficult to breathe.

Each student was allocated a cadaver to work on, working in pairs along with one other fellow student. In Eva's case she shared her cadaver with a girl called Felicity whom she had met before briefly. They were to spend some hours a week together over the next few months carefully dissecting the organs, nervous system, blood supply and so on, of the body of this elderly dead man – Felicity and she affectionately called him 'Bob' – which lay on the stainless steel table in front of them. The dissection sessions were frequently interrupted by jokes and stories from the more jovial male characters in the class, but during the hour long sessions the students never really forgot the seriousness of the task they were involved with, and none of them ever lost their sense of dignity towards the work they were being honoured with. They would enter the dissecting room as a procession of young men and women in an almost reverential way, not unlike a cathedral choir processing in to the nave. The pungent smell of the formalin became less shocking to the system with time, but the serious nature of the dissecting sessions was never really lost on Eva and her colleagues.

Eva passed her pre-clinical exams without difficulty. Life as a clinical medical student – starting the three year apprenticeship on the wards of the new Royal Free Hospital Medical School – was certainly the challenge that she had expected. In spite of its history for admitting women, the new hospital was still male dominated, even after all these years, although there were a number of prominent women among the staff. In addition to this, there was a core of older, not to say elderly, men who had moved from the old hospital who were being challenged for their dominance by bright new consultants and lecturers many of whom now were women. They didn't take kindly to the challenge, Eva found.

Three years later, Eva passed her University of London MB, BS final examination with honours. She was now 'Dr Bruns'. The graduation ceremony was held in the University Senate House on Malet Street. Sitting in the audience proudly supporting her were Rosa and Jürgen. As she mounted the steps and walked along the stage towards the University Vice-Chancellor to collect her certificate she looked down and saw them sitting in the audience, three rows back, beaming broadly at her. Eva could not have been prouder of herself and smiled back happily at them. She knew her own mother would have been proud too, were she still alive to witness the occasion.

CHAPTER 51

1981

Two months after qualifying as a doctor, Eva started work. She spent her pre-registration year working at St Thomas' Hospital, six months in the general surgery department and six months in general medicine. Following that, she decided to apply for a year working as a general practitioner's assistant. She did not think that she wanted to make her life's work in general practice – she had already determined on a more academic career in the long term and had an interest in going into medical research – but she also enjoyed looking after sick patients enormously and had the very sensible idea that it was important that she should experience life at the general practice coal face before she branched out into pastures more esoteric.

She obtained a post working with a single-handed general practitioner in Whitechapel, in the east end of London. It was a complete change from anything she had done before, as a nurse or a doctor. For the first time in her adult life she was exposed to poverty and need in a way which shocked her. Certainly life in Vienna with Rosa and Jürgen, who were a comfortably off professional couple, had never exposed her to such things. Somehow she had previously developed the idea that general practice was life in a slow lane, something that attracted those doctors who might be less ambitious than others. She did not know where this idea had arisen from in her mind – perhaps it was merely that at that time medicine in general was taught exclusively by rather ivory tower professors in academic teaching hospitals, who very likely had never experienced general practice themselves, and where general practice was not really formally included on the syllabus in any meaningful way. Whatever her preconceived ideas might have been, she was very quickly disabused of the idea that working as a general practitioner in the east end of London was an easy option. It presented a considerable challenge for her as a newly qualified doctor with no previous experience in treating society at large, not to mention coping with the poverty and public health issues she was to come across.

One Friday evening Eva was called to see a very ill child at home. By this time she was purposely spending a lot of her time undertaking home visits. She had come to learn that when a doctor was called upon to visit a sick person at home, there was almost always a good reason for this. Patients very rarely called her out without good cause. She found that it was a very instructive way to get to know her patients and their families. She would have the opportunity to obtain an insight into the circumstances of a particular patient, and also to develop a relationship and understanding of the whole family and their situation and needs.

On this particular evening the house she visited was in a very poor, run-down part of the east end of the city, just off the Mile End Road. The house was part of a dilapidated tenement, virtually a slum. The door was opened by a distressed young mother.

'Oh doctor, thank you very much for comin',' the anxious woman greeted her, ushering her in through the battered front door into a hall bare of carpets.

'My little girl's very unwell, with a 'orrible cough. She can hardly get her breaths between coughs.' She led Eva along a passage towards a ground floor room. Even before entering the room, Eva could hear the alarming, screeching whoops coming from inside it. When she entered the room what she saw was an emaciated very distressed little girl lying on a sofa bed, the clothes all dis-arranged. The child's body was being wracked by paroxysms of never-ending coughing, interspersed by violent whooping, such that she was barely able to catch her breath, let alone speak. The mother had told Eva in the hall that Jenny was twelve years old. She looked less than half that age: she was desperately thin and with her stunted growth she was probably not much taller than a well-nourished girl of the age of six would have been.

Eva sat on the bed, talking quietly and reassuringly to the very ill little girl. She took out the stethoscope from her bag and started to examine the girl's chest. Her heart was beating so fast it was difficult to count, it must have been at least more than one hundred and fifty beats per minute Eva thought. Auscultating the girl's chest with her stethoscope, Eva's ears were bombarded by increased noisy wet breath sounds. At that moment, in the middle of a body-wrenching bout of coughing, the little girl shot forward and vomited all over the bed clothes. She collapsed back onto her pillow gasping for breath. Eva gently brushed her long thin hair, which was now matted with vomit, off the girl's face. She turned down the top of the sheet to cover up the vomit.

'It's all right Jenny,' she said. 'It's going to be all right. We're going to make you better.' She walked out of the room to talk to the girl's mother alone.

The very anxious mother walked with her to the front door.

'Jenny is very ill, Mrs Moss. I'm sorry to tell you that I think she has a very bad case of whooping cough. She needs to be admitted to hospital urgently. I'm going to arrange for an ambulance to take her in to the London Hospital up the road. You will be able to go in the ambulance with her.' The mother broke down in tears, worried by Eva's serious tone but at the same time grateful that something was going to be done to help her daughter.

'She's not going to die, is she doctor?' The woman pleaded to her. 'I've already lost two of my kids from the pneumonia, and I couldn't bear to lose Jenny as well. I love her so much!'

Eva felt for the poor young mother. 'It's a very good hospital, Mrs Moss. I am sure the doctors and nurses will do everything they can to look after Jenny and make her well again.

'Thank you for everything you are doing, doctor.' The mother hung desperately on to Eva's arm as she took her leave and left to arrange the little girl's admission to hospital.

Eva remembered the story she had read about Dr William Marsden, and how he had tried to rescue a young girl dying in the street, but failed to be able to help her when none of the hospitals nearby would agree to take her in. 'We have come quite a long way from that,' she told herself, 'but we still have a long way to go.'

CHAPTER 52

1985

Eva sat on a seat in the middle of the back row of the lecture theatre. She had come to King's College London on the Strand to listen to a symposium about prostaglandins which interested her. She had only started her new post at the Hammersmith Hospital earlier that month, working as a research assistant in the department of pharmacology and a clinical lecturer in medicine. She had been given a number of projects to consider, but had not yet decided in what direction she wanted to focus on for her main research topic. She was not being put under particular pressure by her new boss, Professor Steve Docherty, but she was keen to get going. Until she had decided the direction of travel she wanted to take she could not start applying for funding. The life of a clinical researcher depended on attracting grants from one or a number of bodies such as the Medical Research Council or the Wellcome Foundation. Competition for funding was fierce, both within her own institution and from other medical research centres around the UK. And not only her salary but also the salaries of any post-doctorate colleagues she may want to appoint to work with her depended on obtaining sponsorship. Added to which was the need to attract funding for equipment to set up her research laboratory.

The morning session came to a close with the last speaker receiving a round of applause. Eva closed her note book and sat there wondering what she should do in the hour and a half lunch break she had in front of her.

'Hello, my name's Stephan.' The man who had been sitting on the left at the end of her row had slid down the seats and held out his hand to introduce himself.

'Oh, hello. I'm Eva,' she replied. She had been concentrating on the lecture and had not noticed him sitting there before. He must have come in late and slipped in.

'Interesting lecture,' Stephan said. 'Where are you from?'

'I've just started as a research assistant at the Hammersmith. How about you?'

'I'm a lecturer in pharmacology here at King's,' he replied. 'But what I really meant was – where do you come from?'

'Oh, I see. I'm from Hungary originally, but have been living in London for twenty years now. Before that I was living in Vienna.'

'What a coincidence!' Stephan laughed. 'I'm Hungarian too. But I have lived in England for many years as well. I came over as a child with my parents in 1956 when they escaped from the Soviet invasion. What shall we do for lunch?'

They left the lecture room and walked out of the College by the side entrance into Surrey Street. 'There's a nice pub round the corner,' he said, leading her across the road and into a small side street.

The Cheshire Cheese was a 17th century pub on the corner of Little Essex Street, with chamber pots hanging from the ceiling. Entering the rustic building was like going back in time. She could imagine a young Charles Dickens sitting in the corner, smoking a clay pipe and making notes on a sheet of paper for his next story. In spite of being the lunch hour, it was not too noisy – quiet enough to talk – and they sat in front of a cosy fireplace and inhaled the wood smoke. The place seemed to be inhabited by men and women from the legal profession. Stephan explained to Eva that it was one of the favourite haunts for the lawyers and secretaries of the Inner Temple and the legal firms with offices nearby. It was obvious to Eva that it was one of his favourite places too.

The lunch hour flew by. Eva was pleased to have some company and they spent the time talking about their mutual Hungarian roots. Stephan was a softly spoken, polite young man, as intelligent as Eva herself. She found out in their first meeting that in addition to his scientific brain, he liked to play the piano and paint in water colours. They returned to the symposium well fed and watered and only just made the lecture theatre on time for the start of the afternoon session.

As they filed out with the rest of the audience at the end of the afternoon Stephan turned to Eva. 'How about lunch again on Wednesday next week?

I've got a busy time finishing and writing up a project which has to be submitted by next Tuesday, but would free after that.'

'Thank you, Stephan, that would be nice,' Eva said. They shook hands lightly and he turned back towards his laboratory in King's, while Eva made for the tube station. She sat on the underground train feeling happy and a little surprised by the day out she'd had. She had not had a boyfriend as such since being in nurse training school – and since qualifying as a doctor she'd been too busy to develop many friends at all. But she thought he was nice. She was pleased he had wanted to meet up with her again.

* * *

The next Wednesday she left Hammersmith early for lunch, telling her colleagues she would be away for a couple of hours, and took the underground in to central London. She got off at Charing Cross station and walked down Villiers Street to the embankment, strolling along the river to the Temple station, where they had arranged to meet.

Stephan was waiting there to meet her. 'Come on, then, I've decided on some lunch time entertainment.' He strode off back up the road towards the Strand, leaving Eva to follow him.

'Where are we going?' she asked, as she caught up with him, breathing heavily as she rushed up the hill after him.

'You'll see,' he replied.

They turned right and crossed over the road, walking along the Strand. They passed King's College again and came to a stop near the end of the Strand. Eva looked up to see an imposing turreted building in front of them. The ornate painted stone sign announced the Royal Courts of Justice. Stephan almost ran up the steps and held the door open for her.

'Welcome to The Appeal Courts,' he said, guiding her inside with his arm around her and up the stairs to the public galleries. He chose a court at random, and held the door open for her again. They crept quietly in to the back of the public viewing gallery. Eva felt as if she was entering a church. There was a court still in session; three elderly looking appeal judges wigged and fully gowned in red satin with blue diagonal sashes – like something out of the

French Republic, she thought to herself – sat in the centre of the raised dais at the front of the court. Stephan sat down at the end of pew and patted the seat next to him, inviting her to join him.

Eva spent the whole of the lunch hour transfixed by the theatre that was being played out before her. The appeal case they had barged in on was an immensely complicated patent case. The QCs were summing up after apparently some days of the hearing. The case centred on the aero engine company Rolls Royce having sued another company for stealing its design for an aeroplane jet engine, breeching its copyright. Most of the extremely technical jargon was completely over Eva's head, but she found the minutiae of the highly complicated brief that the QCs for both the plaintiff and defence addressed fascinating nevertheless.

While the summing up was proceeding, she noticed that the middle of the three learned judges – presumably the senior judge, who looked like Methuselah – was sitting back in his chair staring at the ceiling, his lower jaw drooping loosely, such that she felt he might start dribbling at any moment. The judge to his right was slumped quite far forward in his seat and, from where Eva could see, appeared to have his eyes shut. 'The poor man's gone to sleep,' she thought to herself in amusement. The summing up by the QCs on both sides was concluded and a recess for lunch was announced.

They stood on the pavement outside, getting some fresh air.

'Have you had enough?' Stephan asked, looking at her.

'Oh no, it's fascinating!' Eva replied. 'I'd never have thought of doing this as a lunch hour entertainment. Stephan laughed: 'I'm glad you're enjoying yourself,' he said. 'I come her quite often in my lunch break. I find it clears the mind, concentrating on something quite different from life and work is a good tonic somehow. The last appeal case I followed was a gruesome murder case which went on for a few weeks. The guy failed in his appeal, in spite of his excellent QC's efforts.

They went back in after the break along with the other members of the public who had been in the viewing gallery with them. Eva was surprised to find that the three judges were ready to deliver their opinions, which each did in turn. They had obviously prepared their judgements in advance. She was even more surprised to hear how erudite and eloquent all three were in their deliveries. They spoke at great length and with an impressive grasp of the very detailed technical discussion that they had obviously taken in as the appeal hearing had proceeded. They read from the notes they had made as the trial progressed. Her admiration for their intelligence and grasp of the subject which they were pronouncing on was equally true for tall three of them, including the very elderly senior judge and the one on his right who had appeared to be asleep during the whole of the summing up. Her assessment of the senior judicial bench went up considerably, in spite of the fact that they had appeared to her as very elderly characters in a comic light opera when she first arrived in the court.

'Thank you so much, Stephan. That was a nice lunch treat,' she said squeezing his hand.

'That's a pleasure,' he said with a laugh. 'And it didn't cost me anything!' he added with another laugh, kissing her tenderly on the cheek.

Eva walked off to her tube station feeling happy. She had meant what she'd said. She had enjoyed herself enormously, in a most unusual way. She started to take Stephan Gyor seriously. She already knew he was a very bright scientist and gifted in other ways. She had to admit that he was also an interesting companion.

It was not long before Eva and Stephan were a couple. They were seeing each other at every opportunity they could find, whenever each of their busy work lives allowed. Eva was very happy; she was in love with Stephan and knew he loved her.

CHAPTER 53

1982

The wedding plans were more or less sorted out. Three weeks before the wedding day, Eva suddenly had a strong urge to visit Poland. By pure chance, the very next day she received a letter inviting her to give a lecture at short notice to one of her collaborating research units at the University Hospital in Leipzig. She dictated her acceptance letter with enthusiasm, asking her secretary on the Dictaphone to go ahead and make the travel arrangements to get her there for the date in question as soon as possible. 'By the way,' she added on an impulse, 'could you arrange for me to fly back to London via Krakow, and book me into a hotel there for three nights. I'd like to have a couple of days to look around. Thanks, Stella.' She signed off her dictation with a smile, surprised with herself that she had taken that decision on the spot, without having made any concrete plans in her head before this. She had not even discussed her strong wish to visit Poland with Stephan, but she was sure that he would be happy with the scheme when he learnt why it was she wanted to go.

The lecture went well and Eva had an enjoyable two days meeting up with her colleague Professor Franz Fischer and members of his team at the Faculty of Ophthalmology in the University of Leipzig. He drove her back to the airport at the end of her two-day visit. Eva and he had worked together for many years and by now and had become good friends.

'Where are you flying to next, Eva?' he said with a smile.

Eva took the joke and laughed back at him. She knew that she travelled so much around the world these days in pursuit of her work, going to conferences, lecturing and visiting other research institutes with the same interests as hers, that her own staff and many other colleagues she met made a running joke of the fact. Her secretary Stella had confided to her while making yet more travel arrangements for her a while ago that the joke that went round was: 'Wherever you are in the world, and whichever airport you are flying in or out of, you will meet Eva Bruns in the transit lounge!' Eva had to laugh. It was almost true, and she knew the joke was made out of affection and admiration for her devotion to her work.

'As it happens,' Eva replied to Franz, 'I'm off to spend a couple of days in Krakow – this time for leisure, not work.'

'I don't believe you,' Professor Fischer laughed, as he opened the door of the car for her in the drop off bay to the departure lounge. 'But have a good time, anyway!' He gave her the mandatory kiss on each cheek, and waved genially at her as he drove off.

As soon as her flight landed at Krakow, Eva hailed a taxi and made straight for her hotel. She was tired from her trip and turned in early.

The next morning she walked out into the busy city centre to look at the tourist shops. She saw posters advertising accompanied coach trips to Auschwitz. She had decided already that she had no need to go 'back' there. But she studied the map on the desk of one of the travel agent's offices and picked up a local bus timetable. She found the bus route she wanted and waited patiently at the bus stop on Rynek Główny square for it to arrive. When the bus turned up, she could see that she was the only tourist on board: the rest of the passengers were clearly locals going about their day-to-day business. She got out her map and showed the young woman sitting next to her where she was heading. In her broken German she asked if the girl could show her where to get off. The Polish girl nodded, telling Eva that the stop was before hers and that she would tell her when she had reached her stop.

Eva got off the bus and gave the friendly girl a wave goodbye as the bus drew away. She looked up and down the road, noting that she had landed in a pretty out of the way farming area, but hoping her map reading had been right. The road was only a few kilometres north of where the concentration camps of Auschwitz and Birkenau were situated. She knew this because the camps featured on many tourists' itineraries and therefore were shown prominently on all maps of the region.

Eva trusted her instinct as well as her map reading, and turned right from the bus stop, up the road as it climbed slightly and to the left. At the top of the incline she came to a farm track which she hoped was the one she was looking for. As she stood looking up the track, she could see a farmhouse a few hundred metres at the top. She started to walk slowly toward the farm, taking in her surroundings as she did so.

When she reached the farmhouse, Eva opened the gate and walked up the path to the front door. She knocked once. After a few seconds the door was opened by an elderly man with tanned skin and a stoop, a man who must have worked for many years on his farm in all weathers, she guessed.

'Are you Peter Leahy?' Eva asked him.

'Yes,' the man replied. 'Can I help you?'

Eva held out her hand to Peter and showed him her mother's battered old corn doll which she always carried with her wherever she went. 'I'm Eva,' she said simply.

'My God!' Peter exclaimed. 'Won't you come in?'

Eva entered the modest farmhouse and sat down in front of the wood burning fire. She knew this was a place where she had spent the early months of her life, although of course she could not remember it.

'You know who I am?' Eva asked him.

'Of course I do, Eva. I never thought we would meet again in my life. How on earth did you find me here?' he asked, amazed to see her.

'My mother talked about you such a lot throughout my childhood and described exactly where your farm was; I knew I would not have much difficulty finding it when the time came.'

'My heart has been opened up by your visit,' Peter said. Eva could see he was near to tears with the emotion of seeing her. 'I have never forgotten your mother, or ceased to love her. I have lived for the day which I thought had become impossible. The day she might choose to come and seek me out. And here you are instead.'

'It wasn't my wish to distress you Peter. It was just something that I knew in my heart my mother would wish me to do when I had the chance.' Eva paused.

'How is Eszter?' Peter asked. 'Please tell me she is alive and well!' Eva had a sense that he had already guessed her reply, had worked out in a flash why it was her sitting there and not her mother herself.

'Eszter died in an accident in 1956, when I was twelve, Peter. We had just escaped from Budapest by train to Vienna, fleeing with hundreds of others just before the Soviets invaded Hungary in October of that year. As we walked together out of the train station in Vienna – celebrating our escape to freedom – she was trampled by a coach and horses as she walked into the bright sunshine of the street. She died instantly.'

Peter bent over, with his head in his hands. He was sobbing uncontrollably. Eva sat quietly where she was, not wanting to intrude on his grief, waiting for him to finish crying. After a while he sat up and wiped his eyes with his shirt sleeves, blowing his nose hard with an old piece of cloth he extracted from his pocket.

'I am *such* a stupid man,' Peter said to her. 'I have loved your mother since the day I met her – I am sure she told you the circumstances of that? – and know I should have been brave enough to go looking for her, to find her in Budapest. But I was always too proud to do so, fearing that her husband Robert would throw me out, or, worse still, that Eszter would not want to see me again now that she had made a new life with her husband, after we had been together for only those few weeks before Robert re-appeared. I was afraid of the humiliation that I would bring upon myself and the suffering it might cause her. I was such a fool.

'Robert was not a good husband to Eszter, Peter. He was constantly drunk and never stopped being angry with her for falling in love with you after you had sought her out and both of you had presumed he was dead. His behaviour towards Eszter was always unreasonable and sometimes even violent. I don't think my mother knew why this was, why he changed so much from the young man she married in1943. She was a very forgiving person, and explained to me once that the only reason she could think of was that he had been irreparably damaged by his time in the forced labour camp, where he was starved, beaten and brutalised. She was sure this must have changed him emotionally, altered his whole personality irretrievably in fact.

'As it was, Robert only stayed with Eva for a few months after you left to come back here. He became more and more violent towards my mother, more and more often drunk, until one night he left her completely and never came back. I was still very young and can barely remember him.'

'If it's any consolation, you should know that Eszter never lost her love for you. Even as a young child, I can remember her talking about you to me; she made no secret of the fact that you were the only man she had ever truly loved. I always remember her talking about you like that, just as I remember her describing the fondness she had had for your parents as well as the description she gave me of this farmhouse. That is why I had no real problem finding you today.'

As Eva told this last bit of her mother's story, Peter started to cry again, openly and uncontrollably this time, shaking with grief. She waited patiently until he was able to speak again.

'What a complete fool I have been, Eva! I'm sixty-five now and still love Eszter, and I always will. Yes, I met and married a girl called Julia and settled down with her here. We had two children together and lived happily enough until Julia died from breast cancer eight years ago. But Julia knew that I had always loved Eszter more deeply than I could her. Indeed, on her deathbed, she encouraged me to go and find Eszter again. "It's never too late," she said to me. But of course it was, even though I did not know that at the time. I did not have the courage even then to follow her permission to go looking for Eszter again. In my arrogance I have ruined the lives of all those I have loved, and not least my darling Eszter. What a complete and utter fool I have been!'

Eva sat dumbstruck. She didn't know what to say to this grieving old man that she knew she had met briefly when she was a very young girl, but who she had not seen since. Nevertheless in one way she felt she knew him well; her mother had spoken to her often when she was a child about her enduring love for Peter. As she sat there listening to his grief and remorse, she couldn't help but feel a deep sadness both for her mother and for Peter. A sadness for a love unfulfilled, for a life lost that could have been so different for them both together.

CHAPTER 54

"Dear Peter,

I am writing this back home in England. I am so pleased I finally made the time to visit you during my recent visit to Krakow. It was something I had been meaning to do for years and I am sorry that it took me so long to get round to it.

I was sad to find that you have been living your life with so many regrets since you and Eszter last saw each other. It made me realise how cruel life can be. You should not continue to blame yourself, or indeed my mother either. I understand now that your continued separation from each other was something that neither you nor Eszter had truly wished for. It was just one of those unkind tricks of fate that from time to time life choses to deal out. The failure of communication that both of you regretted was not something that either of you wanted. It was just something that the war ravaged years and its aftermath dictated. It may be that, in these days of such rapid and constant communication between peoples, this might not have happened if you were both living now. But I am not so sure.

The one thing I do want to stress to you again is that Eszter would be sad to know how you have felt about the situation since you last bade farewell to each other all those years ago. She would not have wanted you to have continued to live your live in a state of mourning for the loss of her love. Even now, if she were still alive, I know she would have kissed you and implored you to accept that your mutual love, intense as it was on both your sides, was always destined to be brief. She would have told you that the fact that a candle flares brightly but is then extinguished by a passing breeze does not make its brief intensity any less real. She would have implored you, even now, to put your grief for the loss of her to one side, in memory of your love for her, and to live your life from now on without the pain and suffering you have continued to endure.

I am passing these sentiments and thoughts onto you since I feel I have a duty to do so as the voice piece of my dear departed mother. I know she would have wanted me to have expressed these sentiments to you and would have agreed with them in full.

Peter, I do hope you can see that what I have written above, on both my own and my mother's behalf, is a tribute to your love for her and a plea for you to have the courage to go forward in life knowing this and finally be free of the burden of regret you have been carrying.

With love and hope,

Yours,

Eva."

Eva sealed the envelope. It was three weeks since she had returned from her visit to Peter. She knew she had to write the letter and that her mother would have been pleased that she had.

* * *

"Dear Miss Eva,

I am Greta, Peter's daughter. I am staying at the farmhouse at the moment. I have just found your letter to my father from two weeks ago. I have read the letter myself, and know I have to write to you in reply. I hope you can understand my writing in English.

It grieves my heart to tell you that my father Peter is dead since three weeks ago. My brother Aleksy called to see how he was – we knew he had been so very low of late – and to help him with the cows. When he arrived at the farmhouse, Peter was nowhere to be seen and the cows unattended to and un-milked. Aleksy finally found him lying on the ground by the barn at the bottom of the second field. He had been dead for some time. We don't know what happened. There had been a strong wind and a piece of the felt covering had come loose from the barn roof. It may be he had been trying to fix it and had fallen. It may also be that he took his own life by jumping off the roof in the state of melancholy and despondency that he had been in. We are so very sad for our father. I have come down from Warsaw to attend to my father's affairs. We are grieving deeply for him.

I know that this will come as a great shock to you. I know this because I have read your letter to my father. Please forgive me for having done so; if you consider this an intrusion on your private thoughts to him, then I apologise sincerely. But having read your heartfelt pleas to him, I know that you would want to hear about the death of Peter and share with us in grieving for him.

With my fondest thoughts. In love,

Yours,

Greta."

Eva laid the letter on her lap and sat in silence. Another tear rolled down her cheek, a message of love for both her mother and her love Peter.

CHAPTER 55

They were married on a Saturday morning in September at the Hammersmith town hall. To Eva's joy, Rosa and Jürgen flew over from Vienna for the occasion as did Stephan's father and sister from Budapest. Stephan's mother had died from cancer only a few months before he had met Eva. It was a long time since Eva had last met Rosa and Jürgen, although of course she had continued to keep in touch with them, especially at Christmas and birthdays. She was so pleased to see them in person again. They were both in their late sixties now, and she couldn't help but be a little shocked by how much they had aged.

They rented a flat in Ealing, near the Broadway, which was convenient for them to get to their work from. They would both leave very early for work, kissing goodbye and heading in opposite directions across London. Very often, on weekdays at least, they would both also arrive home late in the evening. But they got into this routine, knowing that each of them was fulfilling their personal and professional ambitions, involved in work they enjoyed. Eva found herself having to bring work home at weekends, whereas Stephan was happy to potter around and lose himself in his piano playing and water colour painting, both of which he had a passion and considerable talent for. At the same time, he was also happy to look after the housework and do most of the cooking, while Eva was busy with her work, using Saturdays and Sundays to catch up.

Eva's work in particular was going especially well. She had developed an intense interest in the investigation and treatment of certain specific types of eye disease, and early on in her tenure at the Hammersmith Hospital had published a number of significant papers on the subjects she had been studying, summarising her research findings. She was a rising star in the Hospital and was given rapid promotion as a consequence. For his part, Stephan was happy to take his career at a more leisurely pace. This did not mean that he was content to mark time, but he had a true academic's approach to enquiry, intelligently examining his results critically and being prepared to repeat experiments on more than one occasion to satisfy himself that his findings were reproducible and genuine. He was good at teaching and enjoyed the interaction it gave him with the undergraduate students. He was also good at bringing bright junior colleagues on board with him, and his lectures were always enthusiastically well attended.

Another talent Stephan had – one that quite surprised Eva – was that he had an entrepreneurial side to him. He had developed a number of techniques in the production of new drugs and went on to market his ideas and projects to a number of different large international pharmaceutical companies. Indeed, so successful did this side of his work become, that within a couple of years he had set up his own company, renting out a workshop in Brentford and employing a small number of men and women to work there with him. He was not only a bright scientist but also had a flair as a businessman. Eva was amazed and delighted when this side of his work started earning him quite a lot of money, considerably more than his University lecturer's salary, in fact. Before long they had saved enough between them to buy their first house is Ealing. They were both maximally involved in their work, and neither had an inclination or desire to start thinking of having a family. They had discussed this openly with one another on more than one occasion and were in agreement. They were happy to continue as they were without the additional responsibility of bringing up children.

CHAPTER 56

1986

Following the death of Peter, his son Aleksy and his wife Iren moved into his parents' farm. Aleksy and his sister Greta had been equal benefactors in Peter's will, which had apparently been updated just before his death. This was somewhat unusual, and Greta at least had cause to reflect on the fact that it supported the concerns she'd had that Peter was contemplating his own death, even if he had not taken his own life, which she had a feeling might have been the case. But since the two children benefitted from the new will equally, they had no reason to be dissatisfied with it. Indeed, since Greta and Szymon had moved to live and work in Warsaw they told Aleksy immediately that he and Iren should take over the farm at once and continue to run it.

Aleksy had been working as the manager of another farm nearby, and was pleased to have the challenge of taking on his own freehold farm at last. For his part, Szymon had no interest at all in farming and was making a career for himself in the Polish beer trade in the capital. The arrangement suited the brother and sister and their respective spouses well, and they were pleased that the farm, which had been in the hands of their parents and grandparents for many years now, should remain in the family through Aleksy and his wife.

Their first year on the farm for Aleksy and Iren was difficult. It was clear to Aleksy, when he got down to it, that the land had not been well looked after for a few years and he set about putting right the many things that had gone unattended. In addition to that, the farmhouse needed quite a bit of work on it. He waited for the second summer they were living there to start making good the many repairs to the farmhouse buildings that were needed.

Their second harvest had come and gone, and Aleksy and Iren were pleased that it had been a good one. Aleksy had had to employ a couple of local lads to help him with the extra work at harvest time. Shortly after the harvest had been successfully completed, Iren realised that she was pregnant. Their son was born the next spring, in March, 1984. They called him Wilthord.

CHAPTER 57

September, 2005

For the first time since she had fled the city with her mother in 1956, Eva was back in Budapest. She had come as an invited speaker to a European ophthalmology conference. She always enjoyed attending conferences. They gave her a break from work, an opportunity to learn from other colleagues and time to reflect on the progress of her own research in the context of what she had learnt. But this meeting was special for other reasons. She was sixty one now and it was her chance to re-connect with her mother and family and early life. She had arrived in a spirit of excitement and hope that she would find some peace in the city. She had asked her secretary Stella to book her extra time after the conference proceedings had concluded, so that she could use this opportunity to get to know Budapest once more.

During the lunch interval on the first day of the conference, Eva decided to look for her mother's family apartment just behind the basilica. She walked the short distance from the conference hall and found the house without difficulty. She stood on the opposite side of the road for a minute, gazing at it. It was all so familiar: nothing seemed to have changed, even after nearly half a century since she and her mother fled from their home there in the early hours of that October night in 1956, in spite of the fact that she knew that many of the buildings around which had been destroyed in the war had since been completely rebuilt. She crossed the road and pushed at the great maroon front door, which swung open in front of her. She walked through the vestibule and stood at the entrance to the courtyard, which even now she remembered so well. In the far corner on the left was the front door to what had been their apartment. She felt no need to go and knock on it. That would only cause embarrassment to the present inhabitants and to herself.

As she looked across at what had been her childhood home, she saw a young girl with a corn doll in her hand look up and smile at her from the corner of the courtyard. Eva smiled back at the girl, and turned and walked back onto the street. She had done what she had wanted to do.

* * *

The morning after the close of the conference, Eva took the short walk from her hotel into Vörösmarty Square, where a tourist market was in full swing, and from there walked the couple of hundred metres to the banks of the River Danube. It was a warm summer's day and the sunshine was bouncing off the waves made by the pleasure boats that were passing in both directions. She turned right and strolled along towards the Hungarian Parliament building. She felt happy to be back. Although she had only been a twelve year old girl when she left the city with her mother that night in 1956, she could still remember the sights and sounds of the place, which came back to her as she walked.

She passed the imperious, ornate Hungarian parliament building, with its ceremonial guards standing outside looking bored. Turning back down the river, about three hundred metres south of the parliament, between Roosevelt and Kossuth Squares, she saw a huddle of tourists looking at something on the ground by the river bank. She approached the place and stepped between the groups of people to see what they were looking at.

On the ground in front of her, in a long line along the edge of the river bank, she saw scores of pairs of shoes. Except these weren't ordinary shoes. They were shoes made of iron which had been fixed to the stone embankment. They had obviously been created with care by a gifted sculptor. There were pairs of coarse men's boots; of women's shoes and boots of all kinds, including high heeled shoes; and last but not least all sizes of children's shoes, including touching little babies' booties. She could hear the tourists chattering around her in different languages. Apparently this was some sort of Holocaust memorial which had only recently been created. She turned around to see behind her a plaque that had been placed next to the memorial. It read:

IN MEMORY OF THE VICTIMS SHOT INTO THE DANUBE

BY ARROW CROSS MALITIAMEN IN 1944-45

ERECTED 16TH APRIL, 2005

When Eva got back to her hotel she went onto her laptop to read about the memorial. She found out that it had recently been conceived by the film director and poet Can Togay, who'd created it together with the sculptor Gyula Pauer to honour the Jews who were killed by fascist Arrow Cross militiamen in Budapest during World War II. The victims had been ordered to take off their shoes and were shot at the edge of the Danube so that their bodies fell into the river and were carried away. The memorial represents their shoes that were left behind them on the bank. Togay wrote in his description of their creation:

"The composition titled 'Shoes on the Danube Bank' gives remembrance to the 3,500 people, 800 of them Jews, who were shot into the Danube during the time of the Arrow Cross terror. The sculptor created sixty pairs of period-appropriate shoes out of iron. The shoes are attached to the stone embankment, and behind them lies a 40 meter long, 70 cm high stone bench. At three points are cast iron signs, with the following text in Hungarian, English, and Hebrew: "To the memory of the victims shot into the Danube by Arrow Cross militiamen in 1944–45. Erected 16 April 2005."

Eva also read that most of the murders along the edge of the River Danube took place around December 1944 and January 1945, when the members of the Arrow Cross Party police took as many as 20,000 Jews from the newly established Budapest ghetto and executed them, some of these along the river bank in the place where the memorial now stands.

Eva walked away from the beautiful, poignant memorial and the gathering of tourists taking it in. She remembered the story her mother Eszter had told her about the Dutch Jewish lawyer Arno Claussen and his wife Hanneke. Her mother had told her how in 1945 Claussen had been instrumental in helping them survive death from starvation, when he had sought her out and handed over money that her father had placed with him in trust for his daughter Eszter when she reached the age of twenty-one.

Eszter had told Eva that the lawyer and his wife had been working with the Swedish special envoy Raoul Wallenberg to save many Jewish people by sheltering them in 'safe houses'. The Claussens themselves had hidden families from the Nazis by harbouring them before they were passed on to Wallenberg to be transferred to one of these safe houses. She had told Eva that Arno Claussen had been murdered by Soviet troops, perhaps because of his association with Wallenberg. He and many more had been the unsung heroes who had stood up to the brutal Nazi regime and paid with their lives. Wallenberg himself had been detained about the same time and taken to Moscow with his driver. He disappeared in the USSR and was presumed to have been shot himself.

On the plane home the next day, Eva again said a prayer to the unknown god who had saved her and her mother from the Holocaust and had given her a life to live.

CHAPTER 58

'D amn!' Eva cursed to herself.

She was sitting in a darkened room her laboratory in the Hammersmith Hospital, carrying out her research using a laser beam on the diseased retina of the eye. The equipment she still used after all these years was a rather early prototype, but in spite of this it had stood her in good stead for many years and had led to the breakthroughs her research had produced. From time to time, however, when the beam hit the metal side of the slit lamp, she would receive a reflected beam back into her own eye, temporarily causing the vision to black out. 'Damn!' she said again, when she received a second 'shock' in quick succession. She knew she was taking a risk to her own sight, but shrugged it off in her determination to carry on with her research. The use of a light beam to produce light coagulation had been pioneered by the German ophthalmologist Gerhard Meyer-Schwickerath in the late 1940s which had then led to the use of laser coagulation to treat diabetic retinopathy in 1954. Eva had worked to develop the technique to treat the oedema which resulted in the central part of the retina in some patients with diabetes. Since she first began as a research fellow at the Hammersmith she had established a reputation for her expertise with the technique.

It was getting late – although she had lost an exact idea of the time, working as she had been for many hours into the evening – and she knew she should probably call it a day. She packed up her equipment, turned off the lab lights and closed the door behind her. Walking down the poorly lit corridor she had some trouble seeing her way. This was not the first time after receiving laser sparks in one or other of her eyes that she had acquired some blurring of her own vision. And that evening she had received sparks in both eyes. But up to now the blurring of her vision had always been temporary: by next morning her sight had always seemed to have returned to normal. She knew that she had to be careful, that she really should avoid continuing to receive too many more of these sparks into her own eyes. She would ask the engineers in the hospital's electrical department to look at the laser equipment for her again tomorrow.

Stephan was waiting for her patiently in the foyer, sitting on one of the bench seats reading the evening paper which was open on the table in front of him. However late she was packing up for the day, he was always there to meet her from work and never complained about the lateness of the hour. He got to his feet as soon as he saw her, kissed her on the cheek and took her hand. Hand in hand they walked together to the tube station.

* * *

The next day Eva was sitting in her lab thinking over the problem with her equipment. The fact of the matter was that as soon she had woken up that morning she had been aware that the blurring of her vision had not gone away overnight, like it had on previous occasions when she had received laser 'sparks' in her eyes. And this morning she was sitting there with blurred vision in both eyes, not just in one or the other, as had been the case before. She was fully aware of the seriousness of the situation. She knew there was a real possibility that she might be at risk of permanent damage to her eyesight. But she was not prepared to suspend her research because of this. She had reached a critical phase in her experiments, when her results were highly suggestive that the medical use of laser therapy could at least arrest or even reverse the presence of sight-threatening macula oedema and loss of sight in her patients who were suffering from the problem.

But she wasn't there yet. She had to confirm beyond all doubt the effectiveness of this treatment by significantly increasing the number of patients treated, following their progress for a considerable longer time yet, and comparing the outcomes with the other group of patients who had not been offered the treatment at the present, her 'control' group. She would just have to be very much more careful about not exposing her own eyes to accidental 'sparks'. She had to hope that, if she did so, the problem with her vision at present would settle down, as it had done before, and that all would be well with her own eyesight.

'Morning, Dr Bruns.' She looked up and saw the blurred face of Tony, the mechanic from the hospital EME – electrical and mechanical engineering – department.

'Oh, good morning Tony,' she said. 'I'm glad you've come. I've been having more problems with this wretched laser gun. Even after you took a good look at it last week, it's continued to 'backfire'. I don't know whether this has something to do with an electrical short circuit or a mechanical issue. Perhaps there is still a problem with the width of the aperture still being too narrow, which causes the laser beams to reflect back off the chassis from time to time? The fact that you widened the aperture width last time doesn't seem to have helped. The problem has persisted. In fact I had another couple of 'sparks' last night. In both eyes.'

'I'm very sorry to hear that, Dr Bruns. I'll take the whole apparatus back to the workshop and look over it again in detail.' He started to load the laser machine onto a trolley he had brought with him.

'In the meantime,' Tony said as he started to wheel the trolley out of the door, 'I think you should suspend your research using this equipment until we have corrected the problem with certainty.'

'I can't do that!' Eva said. 'I'm at a really critical point in my study. I badly need more patients to treat and more time to follow them and the control group up. I need to get to the point of adequate numbers of study size and statistically significant changes in outcome between the two groups to prove to myself and the outside world that we have a breakthrough in treatment here.'

'I'll do what I can, doctor,' Tony said over his shoulder as he wheeled her equipment out of the door.

CHAPTER 59

September, 2008

va stood behind the lectern, her eyes watering with happiness and gratitude. The audience of five hundred ophthalmologists from around the world in the vast Vienna conference arena in front of her were raising the roof in a standing ovation. She had just delivered the Gold Medal lecture to the International Society of Ophthalmology. This was an honour of the highest esteem. She had herself sat in the audience at previous annual conferences, listening year on year to many of the prominent men and women in her speciality giving their Gold Medal lectures. When she had received the letter nearly a year ago, with the news that she was to be the recipient of the Society's gold medal herself and the invitation to deliver the lecture at the next annual meeting in Vienna, she could not believe it. She had to sit down. When Stephan walked into the room, she picked up the letter from her lap where it lay open and handed it to him.

'Darling, that's wonderful news!' he said bending down to hug her. 'But I am not surprised. Nobody deserves it more. We'll have a celebration trip to Vienna in September!'

In spite of her normally academic *sang-froid* approach to these matters, Eva could not resist feeling a frisson of excitement. In her years as an international researcher she had travelled all round the world delivering papers at academic meetings and conferences, in most of the large cities in all of the continents, including to Hungary, the country of her birth. But, as it happened, she had never before had the opportunity to do so in Vienna. Jürgen and Rosa had both died close to each other in the last couple of years, but much to her sadness she had not been able to attend either of their funerals because of the short notice and her clinical commitments at the time, although she had sent flowers and heartfelt letters of condolence. She still practised under her maiden name as Dr Bruns, the name of her adoptive parents, even after her marriage to Stephan. While this was common practice these days among female doctors, she did so herself partly because of her continued affection and gratitude towards her Austrian parents.

The president of the association gave a valedictory speech of congratulation, placed the gold medal which was hanging from a purple ribbon around her neck, and there was another prolonged session of applause. When it had died down, Eva came down from the stage to be thronged by well-meaning colleagues wishing to congratulate her. She could see Stephan modestly standing in the aisle to the side of the hall, beaming broadly towards her while waiting patiently for those wishing to express their tributes to her had finished. After about twenty minutes all her admirers had given her their congratulations and the last members of the audience were drifting out of the hall. Eva was gathering up her notes and shutting her briefcase as Stephan reached her.

'Darling, that was fantastic!' he said, giving her a big hug.

'Thanks, love,' was all she said to him, but she was grinning with satisfaction and relief. 'Where shall we go for supper?'

'I thought there was a conference dinner tonight. Won't you be expected to go, as the celebrated Gold Medal winner?' Stephan said, with his tongue visibly in his cheek.

'I'm too tired for any more of that,' Eva replied. 'I've already given my apologies for not attending to the President.'

'That's a relief then.' Stephan said, 'because I've already got the evening entertainments arranged.'

'What do you have in mind – a visit to the Austrian Appeal courts?' Eva said, and they both went out laughing.

Stephan had found a small little restaurant in the Mozart district and had booked a table for two which was waiting for them. They sat in front of an open fire, enjoying a glass of champagne, and talking about the day.

'You really did think it went OK?' Eva asked her husband, uncharacteristically hesitant for someone who did this sort of thing on a regular basis.

'Relax!' Stephan ordered her. 'It was perfect. A completely faultless performance in the view of this ignorant theatre critic. Why, weren't you happy with the way it went?'

'It's just that –' Eva hesitated – 'I nearly started on the wrap up summary before I'd delivered the last section of the body of the lecture.'

'Well, I didn't notice. How did that happen?'

'I – I had trouble reading my own slides!' Eva was relieved to get it out.

'What on earth do you mean, dear?' Stephan said.

Eva placed her hand over his across the table. 'For some time now I've been aware that my vision seems to be failing. In both eyes. That's why I bumped into our hotel bedroom door frame yesterday, and have been having regular accidents and scrapes with things at work and home over the past few months.' She still had the nasty bruise on the left side of her forehead and temple from the door frame, although it had been dark enough not to be noticed in the artificial light up on the stage from where she had been delivering her lecture.

'Oh, bugger! Why haven't you mentioned this to me before?' he said, looking alarmed at her. It was very unusual for Stephan to swear.

'It has been difficult to accept this possibility myself. I suppose I have been suppressing the fact in the hope it might go away, just like many of my patients do when faced with their own failing sight.'

'Well, we need to get you seen by somebody as soon as we get back,' he said, squeezing her hand hard. 'We need to get you examined by an expert who can tell us the cause of the problem and how it can be treated.'

CHAPTER 60

Eva was sitting in the front room of number 6 Park Square West, the house of Mr Julian Kingsley-Woolf, the eminent ophthalmic surgeon from the Westminster Hospital, whom she had come to consult. He ran his lucrative private practice from his home, and this was his consulting room. Although she had never met him, as far as she was aware, Eva had been attracted to him not so much because of his reputation as an ophthalmologist – which she knew of from his papers and the high opinions that many of her colleagues had of him – but because of what she had heard of the other side of him, which she found fascinating. Mr Kingsley-Woolf had a keen interest in the arts and architecture in particular, which was reflected no less in the line of elegant stuccoed terrace houses along this side of Park Square West, situated just south of Regent's Park, in one of which he lived. The terrace had been built by John Nash in the 1820s.

Kingsley-Woolf had been close to the Bloomsbury group of artists and writers and she had been told that the artist Duncan Grant was living in his basement at the moment. In addition to his love of the arts and reputation as a leading ophthalmologist, he was also a pioneer gay rights activist, one of the first people in the United Kingdom to come out as openly gay, and had played a leading role in the campaign to repeal the UK's anti-gay laws. He had been one of three prominent homosexual men who had bravely given evidence to the Wolfenden Committee, testimony which helped persuade the Committee to recommend to Parliament that male homosexuality should be decriminalised, which had finally been achieved in 1967.

'Eva. Do come in.' Julian Kingsley-Woolf appeared through a curtain from the back room. Eva looked up and, with her blurred vision, could just make out a long oval face with eyes beaming benignly over gold half-rimmed spectacles which sat low on his nose.

'Pleased to meet you, my dear,' he said in an avuncular fashion, which Eva did not mind, as he stepped forward to shake her hand. He then took Eva kindly by the hand and led her through to his consulting room which led off the waiting lounge. Eva followed him readily, not only because she needed his guidance into the dimly lit room, but also because she somehow already felt greatly reassured in his presence. He sat her down on what appeared to be a piano stool covered by a red satin cushion, her hands resting lightly on the table in front of her. On the table was his ocular examination equipment.

'How long have you been having problems with your vision, my dear?' Julian asked.

'It's difficult to say,' Eva replied. 'It's been coming on gradually. But probably for a few months at least. Initially I thought it was something to do with needing reading glasses, but more recently I have had difficulty seeing the detail in people's faces and even getting around safely. The optician who referred me on to you sold me a pair of extremely expensive spectacles, but they made no difference whatsoever.'

Kingsley-Woolf snorted at this last piece of information. He was known to be waging a war against high street opticians who sold unnecessary glasses – unnecessarily expensively – to people who only needed simple reading specs. It was against the law for the large chains like Boots to sell reading glasses 'off the peg', which in his opinion was completely unreasonable, and particularly unfair to those with little means.

Mr Kingsley-Woolf guided Eva forward to settle her chin on to the chin rest of his slit lamp, her forehead supported by a concave bar above it.

'I was at the Vienna conference in September and enjoyed your Gold Medal lecture immensely,' Kingsley-Woolf said to her as he made her comfortable. 'Fascinating work, and very exciting for the treatment of maculopathy in the future.'

'Thank you, Julian' Eva replied.

For the next few minutes he scanned the light backwards and forwards over both her eyes, from time to time giving her instructions to 'Look up'; 'Look down'; 'Look left'; 'Look right'. After a while, he asked her to sit back from the slit lamp in order for him to place some fluorescein dye drops into each eye, before continuing his methodical examination. She blinked, as the drops made her eyes smart a little. Having finally finished his examination, he sat back from the lamp and invited her to do the same. 'All done,' he said.

There was a pause while doctor and patient sat looking at each other, waiting for one or other to speak. Eva was the first to do so.

'What did you find, Mr Kingsley-Woolf? What is your diagnosis of my problem?'

Kingsley-Woolf leant forward and placed his hand gently over hers. 'You have developed damage to the macula – the central light receiving part of the retina – in both eyes, my dear.' (They both knew that it was unnecessary for him to explain this to her, as a fellow ophthalmologist, but like all good doctors he knew the importance of not talking in jargon and using simple terms, even when speaking to a doctor colleague who was also a patient.) 'I fear this may have been caused by damage from the lasers that you have been using on your own patients over many years'.

In her heart Eva had already known that this would be the case. She had known it for a long time. 'What treatment can you offer me?' she asked directly, already knowing the answer to her own question as well.

Kingsley-Woolf was always kind but equally always honest with all his patients: 'I am sorry to say that the damage is irreversible. We can give you help with low reading aids, such as illuminated strong magnifying lenses. It goes without saying that you should not expose yourself to any further accidental insult from laser beams to your eyes. The one positive fact is that the marginal retinae are still healthy – your peripheral vision will remain preserved. This will mean that you can still retain some independence, walk around on your own without bumping into things too much if you are careful, even if faces are blurred and reading and fine vision are difficult. What we call your 'pilot' or 'navigational' vision should be preserved.'

Eva walked slowly out of number 6 Park Square West, somehow being more aware of the need to tread more cautiously than she had been when coming in, now that the cause of her deteriorating vision had been confirmed. Looking across Park Square, she could still see the famous tulip tree in bloom in the middle of the gardens, but its details were distinctly blurred. Standing high over her right shoulder, she could also pick up the silhouette of a large birch tree, which was casting its shadow over her where she stood. She made her way carefully back to Great Portland Street tube station.

* * *

Mr Kingsley-Woolf was as good as his word. Within a few days of seeing him, Eva had received a visit from a low vision helper who had provided her with a huge magnifying glass with an inbuilt light on its own stand, which she could place on her desk or the table next to where she was sitting. She found this a great help with improving her fine vision, especially when reading. The first book she started to read was *The World Through Blunted Sight. An inquiry into the influence of defective vision on art and character* by Patrick Trevor-Roper.

CHAPTER 61

May, 2014

It was Eva's seventieth birthday. She couldn't really grasp the fact. She didn't feel any older in her mind than she had when they were first married. She felt that she was as mentally as alert as she had ever been. There was so much talk in the media these days about the rising rates of dementia in our ageing society, but Eva had no fears about this as far as she was concerned. She couldn't explain why, if you asked her. It was just that she had an inner confidence in her own abilities and she was not prepared to allow the threat of age-related problems deter her from her agenda. Her work on the effective use of laser therapy in the treatment of sight-threatening macula eye disease had been concluded, and she had now received the accolades she knew she deserved for pressing on and finishing these studies. But there was so much more that she wanted to achieve before her time was up. She was still working as hard as ever on follow-up research projects, including a number of exciting new avenues of enquiry that she had uncovered. She was in no mood to retire from her professional life and certainly not from her research.

She sat in her armchair in their apartment considering the future. Although it was a Friday, Stephan had persuaded her to take a day off at least to celebrate this special anniversary, and they were booked to go to a musical concert given by the Budapest Symphony Orchestra at the Royal Festival Hall on the South Bank that evening. As she sat relaxing with nothing special to do for a change she was listening to Stephan playing a Liszt sonata in the music room next door. He had left the door between the rooms open so that she could listen. He was playing exquisitely, especially for her. And earlier that morning, over breakfast, he had presented her with the latest watercolour painting he had completed. She knew he had been working on this for some weeks, but he had not allowed her to take a look at it while it was work in progress. He had told her it was a 'secret'.

Eva sat there listening to Stephan's beautiful piano playing. She was very happy to be there with him as he played. But in the back of her mind she was still very concerned about her failing sight. She was unable to banish the worry that she had about whether this was going to progress and how quickly, in spite of Mr Kingsley-Woolf's reassurance to her that she would retain her general vision and therefore some independence. When Stephan had given the completed painting to her lovingly earlier that morning she had thanked him profusely and said how wonderful it was. Perhaps the best painting he had ever painted. It was a portrait of herself, sitting in her favourite chair – the one she was sitting in now, that he had bought her a year or two ago – in the sunshine that was streaming in through the bay window of the sitting room of their apartment. But, although she did not admit the fact to Stephan, she could see the general theme of her portrait, but had been unable to make out the detail clearly.

Eva knew she had to accept the inevitable, whatever that was to be. There was no use fighting it, no use becoming angry and bitter. In any event, she reflected, this burden was but nothing compared to the inhumanity and premature death her countrymen and women had been subjected to in the Holocaust. A fate from which she had been lucky enough to escape. She had to continue to be grateful for this and for the seventy years of life her escape had given her.

CHAPTER 62

Eva sat in her lab at the Hammersmith Hospital late into the evening. Both her senior colleagues and her husband had tactfully suggested on more than one occasion that perhaps the time had come for her to retire from laboratory work. But she wasn't ready to pack up what she loved doing, and was good at. In addition to the work still to be completed, she had recently embarked on a couple of new projects which, depending on how they panned out, were likely to take a number of years to come to fruition. In response to the pressures from the others, she had given up all of her administrative and teaching duties, and she was not taking on any further post-doc colleagues to work with her and to mentor. She was working on on her own now. She had also given up attending conferences and indeed anything that involved long distance air travel. She had to smile wryly to herself when she had come to this decision. 'The rest of the pack will have to miss seeing me in the transit lounges as they pass by on their own travels,' she had said with a laugh to her secretary Stella, who at least had remained loyally at her post with her, after all these years.

Eva finally finished her work for the day as it was getting dark. As she came out of her lab into the reception room she saw that Stephan was not there waiting for her. That was unusual, because he always made a point of getting off work himself in plenty of time to be there to meet her. He would sit patiently waiting for her, whatever time it was she finished. She hesitated, looking up and down the corridor, but then remembered something he had said to her as they both left for work that morning. Something about having to attend an evening seminar, which might go on till quite late, but that he would leave early from it if necessary to make sure he was there to meet her. He must still be delayed, she decided. She would make her way to the tube station by herself. She would probably meet him on his way to pick her up, in which case she would have saved them a few minutes getting home.

She walked down Du Cane Road on the way to White City tube station. It was already dark and she walked cautiously, being careful to avoid the humps in the pavement which surrounded the plane trees which grew at regular intervals along the pavement. The trees had large roots many of which were growing upwards towards the surface in the areas around the trunks. The council did its best to cut the most dangerous bumps down to pavement level, and to asphalt around them – not least to reduce the injuries and law suits from vexatious members of the public who filed them – but they could not spend all day treating the thousands of trees in the borough which needed attention every year. In any case, Eva loved the trees and always thought they were both an attractive feature of the inner city as well as being environmentally important in helping to control the carbon dioxide levels in the air around them.

She reached the corner of the road where Du Cane Road met Wood Lane. She looked up the road in the direction of the tube station, expecting to see Stephan in the distance, hurrying towards her. As she peered up the road, for a split second, she forgot to take care where she was walking. It was completely dark by now, and with her failing eyesight she had been taking special care where she walked until then. In an instant, her foot tripped on the elevated root of a tree at the corner of the road and she fell forward on her face, landing hard on the kerbside. She had not been concentrating, and as a result was not expecting the fall; she'd had no time to take evasive action, to throw her arms out to cushion her landing. As she fell, her body twisted to the right and landed like a dead weight on to the kerb. She felt her right hip crack loudly under the force of her body. She cried out in pain, and lay in the gutter, her breath having been taken out of her by the fall and the resulting intense shaft of pain. She was unable to move.

Eva lay where she was for what seemed an age. In reality, it was only a few minutes before Stephan appeared running towards her. 'Oh. My Darling!' he cried. 'What have you done?!' He pulled off his overcoat, rolled it up and very gently placed it under her head. He stooped there over her at the roadside, wiping the sweat off her forehead with his handkerchief and desperately looking up and down the road for someone to help them.

'Don't worry, Gov,' I've just called for the ambulance. A red faced man in a cloth cap ran over from the other side of the road to re-assure him. Within about ten minutes, an ambulance arrived with its blue flashing light on. The paramedics took over, placing Eva on the stretcher and carefully transferring her into the ambulance, before driving Eva and Stephan the short distance back up the road to Hammersmith Hospital from where she had only just come.

CHAPTER 63

All that night Eva lay rigid in a hospital bed, in the hospital where she had been working for the last twenty-five years. She was unable to move because of the pain in her right hip which was unbearable, in spite of the morphine which the orthopaedic doctors had prescribed and the nurses were injecting at regular intervals into her veins. She lay drifting in and out of sleep as terror dreams washed over her in waves.

She was lying on the floor of a cattle wagon, a baby in her distressed mother's arms. The overpowering smells around her were impossible to bear. The smell of human excrement, as well as the asphyxiating smells of infection and the putrefying smells of the dead human corpses which lay all around them were suffocating her mother and herself. She was a baby, too young to have learnt to talk yet, but already conscious enough of the world around her to be aware of the repulsive smells of the dead and dying which were all around her and her young mother whom she clung to.

The dreams faded for a while, although the pain in her hip never left her. Every so often a well-meaning nurse would bend over her and pose the question: 'How would you rate your pain on a scale of one to ten, Eva?'

How could she possibly answer this question, she asked herself in her semi-conscious state? Even if the pain of a hip fracture could be facilely measured on an arithmetic linear scale – which she herself doubted – in what way would it ever be possible to calculate the weight of human suffering that had been dealt out in the Holocaust by evil men to their brothers and sisters and children in mankind? The suffering that had found its core in the inhuman rendition that was played out in the killing factories of the concentration camps of Auschwitz and Birkenau, from which she and her mother had so remarkably escaped. Her nightmares sprang to life again at this point, and she re-lived the fear and terror of being thrown around in her mother's arms as she sprinted away from the evil railhead of Birkenau, through the electrified wire, across the rocky ground, into the bushes and away through the trees. In Eva's dreams they lay there together in mortal fear in the cold and damp of mildewed leaves in a ditch, waiting for the Alsatian dogs or capture and gunshots that they were sure would come, and

the violence that would end their days and their life together before it had only
just begun.

'Ten! Ten! Ten!' Eva screamed at the well-meaning nurse in answer to her
question, before she fell back into unconsciousness again.

Later on – was it day or night? – the pain and the terrors surfaced again as
her sedation began to wear off, and her conscious level rose to near the surface.
This time, she was sitting on the side of the road, watching as her mother lay on
the kerbside where she had fallen and was bleeding profusely from between her
legs. Eva fell back into unconsciousness – whether because of the pain or the
drugs she was being given in an attempt to control it – only to surface to another
dream of semi-consciousness. Sometime later – she had no idea how long later,
for she had lost all sense of earthly time – she was again sitting on the roadside
in a foreign city observing her mother who was lying there in front of her. But
this time it was different. This time the blood was seeping from her mother's
head. This time, her mother was dead.

CHAPTER 64

The next morning Eva lay in her hospital bed with her eyes closed. The pain in her right hip had been execrable, but was now at last controlled to a smoother level by the regular morphine injections she was receiving – as long as she didn't move her leg, that is: any slight movement caused a searing pain in her hip which, when it came, was frankly something which she was unable to stand without crying out. She was at least conscious, and able to recall the events which had brought her to where she now lay.

She was aware of the presence of people around her bed, talking in medical jargon. The orthopaedic house surgeon was presenting her case to the consultant surgeon and the rest of his team. She could hear him discussing the nature of her injury and the X-ray findings of a severe comminuted hip fracture. Her hip had been crushed into multiple small bone splinters by the fall. She could hear other voices, apparently discussing the possible technical approach surgery would require and the significant risks of surgical intervention. There was a pause in the conversation during which the orthopaedic surgical team was either considering the options or looking at X-ray films, or both.

'I am not sure what Mrs Brun's quality of life is . . .' she heard the young house surgeon enter the conversation again. He was obviously querying whether she might have advanced Alzheimer's disease, and whether it might be kinder for them to not to take the risk of surgical intervention, but to let nature take its course.

To his considerable surprise, Eva opened her eyes and looked straight into the young man's face. 'If you're labelling me a dement, young man, I can assure you I am *not* "one of them". I'm just old and going blind!'

'Put Dr Bruns on the list . . .' said the consultant orthopaedic surgeon, giving Eva a hint of a wink – even though Eva could not see it – as he moved on to the next bed. The young doctors around him had not even realised that their patient was a qualified doctor herself, let alone an internationally known senior researcher in their own hospital.

* * *

The orthopaedic registrar was sitting next to her bed reading from a form he held closely in front of her face, aware of her problem with failing vision. He pointed out with the tip of his ball point pen each line of the document as he read it to her. Not that she could really see it from where she lay; she couldn't sit up properly because of the pain she was in.

'Do you understand the details of the operation we are proposing to undertake, Mrs Bruns?' he said, after reaching the end of the form.

'Yes,' she replied weakly.

'And do you also understand the risks of this surgery – which include bleeding, infection and a chance of death?'

'Of course,' Eva murmured back.

The surgeon guided her hand as she scrawled her name on the bottom of the paper, holding the consent form right up close to her face, so that she could see where to place her signature.

Some time later the porters came for her. She was placed on a trolley, the pain of the move causing her to cry out in spite of their gentleness and kind words.

She lay looking up at the huge ceiling light above her in the anaesthetic room, like an illuminated underbelly of a gigantic mushroom, shining beams of light into the dark cavern in which she lay. The anaesthetist's face came into view above her, his mask over his nose and mouth, as he leaned over close to her to explain what was about to happen.

'I'm just going to place a small cannula into the back of your hand here,' he said kindly.

'And now an injection that will put you to sleep in a few seconds.'

* * *

The next thing Eva remembered was regaining consciousness in a hazy, indistinct fashion.

'Can I get you anything, Eva?' a kind student nurse was asking her.

'No thank you, nurse,' she replied in a croaked whisper, her mouth and throat as dry as a leaf. 'What day is it,' she asked the nurse. 'It's Friday,' the nurse replied. 'You had your operation three days ago.'

Eva drifted in and out of consciousness. When she did wake, her conscious periods were interrupted by waves of rigors as fever wracked her body. She could hardly breathe. In spite of her fever, the terrors seemed to have left her and she felt strangely at peace. She was aware of the doctors at her bedside placing their cold metal stethoscopes on the side of her chest and listening to her lungs. She could hear them discussing the fact that she had developed post-operative pneumonia.

Her pain was gone now. She drifted gently back into a deep sleep once more. The old corn doll of her mother's that she had kept safely with her all these years since her mother's death, which she had brought with her into hospital, fell slowly from her hand to lie on the sheet next to her.

This time, she didn't wake up.

CHAPTER 65

October, 2014

As soon as he heard the news of Eva's death in England, Wilthord took two week's leave from his post as tour guide at Auschwitz-Birkenau and flew from Krakow to London. He had made contact with Eva some years before, having heard about her through his aunt Greta, and had subsequently visited Eva and Stephan in London. During that visit she had told him the remarkable story of the meeting of his grandfather Peter and her mother Eszter and their lifelong love for each other. He'd kept in contact with Eva since that meeting, had come to think of her as his 'great aunt'.

When he arrived in London, Wilthord found his 'uncle' Stephan beside himself in grief. Being the only other close acquaintance of Eva's – her adoptive Austrian parents Rosa and Jürgen Bruns having both died in Vienna some years before – he took it upon himself to arrange her funeral. The funeral director he appointed had asked him tactfully whether he wished for a rabbi to be in attendance. Wilthord declined the offer, explaining politely that, although his 'great aunt' was of Jewish descent, she had lived her life as a non-practising Jew – as indeed had her mother before her and himself, come to that. He chose the readings and music for the service that he felt would be most appropriate.

Eva's funeral was held one afternoon in October in the chapel of Highgate crematorium. There were a large number of people in attendance, friends and former work colleagues of Eva. Standing quietly at the back, hand in hand observing the proceedings, was a couple who nobody else present recognised. They had walked in off the street and, when they realised that a service was about to start, they entered the chapel. As they passed the table in the vestibule, the man paused, picked up a service sheet and showed it to his wife. They stood there and read the front page together in silence:

In Loving Memory of

Eva Bruns

1944-2014

Escapee from Birkenau

A Survivor of the Holocaust

The couple nodded to each other in tacit agreement and slipped in to a pew at the back of the chapel.

The congregation was asked to stand, awaiting the arrival of the coffin. Wilthord was in the front row of the congregation next to his 'uncle' Stephan. In the silence that followed he stood with his head bowed, remembering his 'great aunt' Eva. Since their first meeting, he had always thought of her as somehow different. She had certainly lived her life to the full; she had stood out as unique from those in the crowd around her, as far as he was concerned. He remembered the amazing story she had told him about how the young woman and her baby child – Eva and her mother Eszter – had had a miraculous escape from the railhead at the entrance to Birkenau concentration camp, to where they had been transported by train with hundreds of other Jews from Budapest. And how they had therefore escaped a violent and horrible death – a death which was to be the fate of Eva's mother's father and mother, sister and aunt and millions of other Jews, Roma and disabled peoples.

Wilthord knew only too well the story of all those other deaths. He had devoted his life to telling that story to the thousands of visitors who thronged inquisitively every day to the site of the camps. It was a story he now repeated every day of his life to those who wanted to hear it, in the hope that its history would never be forgotten, from now to eternity. He was determined to continue doing his part, to continue telling the story so that it should never be erased. The facts were so abhorrent that the memory of what happened there to millions of people should never be expunged in the history of time. But it was a death which Eszter and Eva at least had escaped from, to live out their own lives in full in the knowledge of what had occurred to the others who had not had their chance to live.

The coffin arrived, carried reverently by members of Eva's research team, men and women who had the highest regard for their departed senior colleague and friend. Placed on the top of the simple coffin there were no flowers but there was a small branch from a birch tree; under the shadows of these trees Eva had lived her life. Lying below this was a faded, desiccated corn doll which had followed Eszter and Eva in their remarkable journey through their lives. A journey which was nearly terminated before it had begun, but which they had made with courage and determination at all times, in the knowledge of the chance of life that they had both been given.

As the service progressed, Wilthord knew that his 'great aunt' Eva had lived a good life. She had made the very most of the chance of the life which fate had gifted to her at the entrance to Birkenau. She had died peacefully in hospital, from pneumonia following a fractured hip, rather than from the violence of the gas chamber or from the machine gun bullets, the sounds of which were ringing in her ears as her mother fled the scene like a hunted hare with her baby Eva in her arms.

At the end of the service the sound of a cello playing Bruch's *Kol Nidre* rose beautifully towards the ceiling, and the curtains opened to receive the coffin containing Eva's remains into the safe arms of the furnace of the crematorium. It was a civilised end to her being, and one that was in stark contrast to that which might have occurred in another furnace some seventy years earlier.

As the congregation filed out at the end of the funeral service, Stephan and Wilthord stood in the vestibule shaking hands with all those that had attended and thanking them for coming. The man and the woman waited patiently at the back of the line. As they reached Wilthord, the man stepped forward to shake him by the hand. 'My wife and I are sorry for your loss,' he said.

Wilthord took the man's hand and replied: 'Thank you so much, Sir.' Then, blinking at the man and woman as he did so, 'Have we met before?' he asked them, unsure who they were.

'Yes,' the man replied, 'we were in one of your groups when we visited Auschwitz-Birkenau in April.'

'Why, yes,' Wilthord nodded, looking at them both carefully. 'I do remember you now.' The man and woman bowed to him appreciatively in affirmation.

The couple turned away and smiled quietly to each other. They walked back out into the road hand in hand, to continue their afternoon stroll in the autumn sunshine.

POSTSCRIPT

In December 2018 I was concerned to read of the disowning by the Auschwitz Memorial Research Centre of a novel that had been set in Auschwitz which was perceived to be so unauthentic as to be a stain on the memory of the truth.

In the Shadows of the Birch Trees is a work of fiction. An imagined story of one young woman and her baby who may have been lucky enough to escape the horror of the mass murders that were being committed within the extermination camps of Auschwitz-Birkenau as they were about to enter there. The characters in the story bear no relation to anyone living or dead.

The portrayal at the beginning of *In the Shadows of the Birch Trees* of the contemporary couple's visit to Auschwitz-Birkenau was exactly that – the visit that I and my wife paid to the concentration camps in April 2014. I was profoundly moved by my visit to Auschwitz-Birkenau, more so than I could ever have predicted. Out of the glimpse we had of the unimaginable abhorrence of the killing structures that had been created there – unimaginable in the telling without having even a sliver of knowledge about what the living and dying really must have been like – I formed the idea of creating the story of a mother and child who, by an extraordinary twist of fate, escaped this death and lived to lead the lives which were given to them as a result. You may consider me naïve, but I asked myself: 'But what if one, just one, of the prisoners who arrived on the death train had had the chance to escape? What would they have made of the life this reprieve had given them?'

In no way do I, the writer of this story, seek to pretend that I was there at the time of the mass murders or could speak for any of those that were.

***